"PITTSBURGH;
SINS, LIES AND UNTOLD CRIMES."

The way it was.

By Roy Zattiero

Note for Librarians: A cataloguing record for this book is available from Library
and Archives Canada at www.collectionscanada.ca/amicus/index-e.html

Printed in Victoria, BC, Canada.

ISBN: 978-1-4269-0799-9 (sc)
ISBN: 978-1-4269-0800-2 (dj)
ISBN: 978-1-4269-0801-9 (e)

*We at Trafford believe that it is the responsibility of us all, as both individuals and
corporations, to make choices that are environmentally and socially sound. You, in
turn, are supporting this responsible conduct each time you purchase a Trafford book,
or make use of our publishing services. To find out how you are helping, please visit
www.trafford.com/responsiblepublishing.html*

*Our mission is to efficiently provide the world's finest, most comprehensive book
publishing service, enabling every author to experience success. To find out how to
publish your book, your way, and have it available worldwide, visit us online at
www.trafford.com*

Trafford rev. 6/15/2009

 www.trafford.com

North America & international
toll-free: 1 888 232 4444 (USA & Canada)
phone: 250 383 6864 ♦ fax: 250 383 6804 ♦ email: info@trafford.com

The United Kingdom & Europe
phone: +44 (0)1865 487 395 ♦ local rate: 0845 230 9601
facsimile: +44 (0)1865 481 507 ♦ email: info.uk@trafford.com

Disclaimer

"Pittsburgh;

Sins, Lies and Untold Crimes"

This book is written as a novel. Having this been said many of the facts are totally true and based on verifiable issues. Names, dates and institutions have been changed or altered to protect the innocent. No part of this novel is intended to harm or injure any person or entity, except to disclose the truth.

Most authors utilize facts and personal knowledge to formulate their writings. "Sins of Pittsburgh" is no exception. Although considered a historical novel, a few simple alterations could change this books true identification to qualify as a non-fictional publication.

Cover and photograph by Cas Zattiero.

Drawings and sketching by Mason Jones Jr.

Edit and proofread by Dr. William Hoebler, PhD, M.B.A., M.B.S., B.S., B.A., Z.I.A.

Authors' note and apology:

In order to retain the integrity of this book several edits, proofs and recommended changes by Dr. Hoebler were not implemented.

Introduction

"Pittsburgh;

Sins, Lies and Untold Crimes"

In the mid 1800's, the Sisters of Mercy for the Roman Catholic Church based in Maryland were blessed with the task of establishing homes of refuge for young girls without parents. The sisters were dispatched from Emmetsburg to venture north and westward to achieve their Godly duties. Little was given to assist their orders except the powerful hand of the most influential congregation in the world. Cost, money and expenses would have to be obtained by each of the local dioceses where each orphanage would be located. Funds would be gathered from contributions and other activities which were to be implemented at the discretion of the Sisters of Mercy.

There was nothing sinister or underhanded in this endeavor. Every intention was well above board. Motivations were saintly in nature with no other agendas. The board of Bishops had good cause and honorable reasons for ordering this venture. In Europe the Roman Catholic Church was under siege from the Protestants, Lutherans and the Russian Orthodoxy. The mighty Ottoman Empire was also expanding the Muslim faith. Even in America; split away groups such as the Quakers and the newly formed Mormons in New York were gaining strength in the land of the free. In addition to the church's wish to retain its powerful position, other outside worldly factors came to have a direct impact on the Sisters of Mercy mission.

1845 was the worst of the Irish potato failures. This staple of Great Britain in general and Ireland in particular had a devastating effect on over eight million people. Millions of Irish fled the famine for America. Many were in poor health prior to their departure. Nearly all were of the Catholic faith. King Cholera had also long been a prevalent European killer. Now influenza, typhoid and dysentery were advancing unchecked. Hepatitis, T.B., and Scarlet Fever were above the commoners defenses. As many as one in five passengers to the new world would never reach their destination. Millions of Irish would flee while hundreds of thousands would die.

English Parliament further complicated the problems in 1846 with a "Corn Law", over taxing crops at the same time that the French economic depression produced huge amounts of unemployment, social unrest, riots and unprecedented food shortages. Furthermore the Italians staged a major rebellion in Milan during 1848, in their attempt to oust their Austrian masters. Life in Europe was contentious to say the least. Dangerous at best. Good life, security and health were rare. Freedom was sought but elusive.

From America the beautiful came word of the 1849 gold rush. Jobs, food, money, wealth and all the freedoms of life were there for the asking. With the great influx of people came the displacement of children. Parents died on the tough voyages as did others from the diseases that they brought with them. A decade later the American Civil War would also add thousands of parentless children to the roles of unwanted, uncared for and in dire straits.

All of this was happening while at the same time black gold in two forms was being taken from Mother Earth in Pennsylvania and the tri-state area. To dig the coal out of the ground and drill the oil, billions of cheap man hours were required. No one worked harder than the Italian or Irish immigrants, who were easily exploited to the raw bones of their bodies.

The provision of food, education, religious upbringing and the most basic human needs for so many displaced children was without question

a noble and righteous calling during such a time of need.

Its implementation, misuse and predatory sanctuary are a matter of record.

One must never forget that while coal was king and was required for heat and energy, the iron ore to make the steel also had to be taken from the earth. The same earth diggers that are a subject of this book, who dug the coal also mined iron, manned blast furnaces and transported the materials by rail, wagon and river.

May all their hearty souls rest in peace.

Andrazza, in the Italian Alps

Chapter I

· Andrazza – The Italian Alps ·

Far north of mainstream Italy are the majestic Alps. Annual winters here may reach snow fall levels totaling in the hundreds of feet. Summers are short and air is very thin. Residents are the hardest of workers. Masons and miners by trade, the men had to migrate south to Milan, Trieste or Florence for winter income as there would be no work in the snow bound villages of the highlands. For weeks, and often months, it was nearly impossible to even exit the homes of Andrazza. Snow caves from house to house were commonplace. This isolation also contributed to the making of large families.

Homes here are family treasures and are rarely, if ever, sold. Most have been in the same sir name for hundreds of years. Relatives would always join in the construction of a family member's house. The skilled stone masons and crafted carpenters built excellent structures with three or four foot solid stone walls. Beams supported by huge boulders and central fireplaces radiating to all four sides. They were (are) large multi story homes built to withstand the worst of climatic conditions as well as to protect not only the initial family but also generations to come. Architecture was (is) also different then we know it today. The ground floor was not a garage or family room, but rather kept the farm animals which had to be indoors from the freezing winter elements. This gave off additional body heat which helped warm the rooms above. Along with the heat came the constant foul odors. Today's American fireplaces are built on the outside walls for structural and safety reasons. This is not so in the highlands.

By building the house around the fireplace every room received radiant heat and warmth from ventilators. Elders' rooms were closest to the hearth while the youngsters were upstairs or on the far side of the homes center.

As the families grew, so did the house. Solid, well laid stone foundation allowed multi levels to be added. Marshall's home of five stories high plus a steep pitched roof was not uncommon. Generations lived together in close unity. There were no homes or care facilities. The family always cared for itself. The high steep pitched roofs were required for the heavy snow.

Large remote farms were few while the small villages dotted with medium size productions common. Trading commodities by resident's stores was (is) a regular business. Goats milk for wool, pork for produce and wine for bread are still traded to this very day although the Euro has now muddied the waters.

Dense forest surrounded the Italian village. Generations had cut the great timber for their homes, furniture and other needs such as bridges and churches. Each family held claim to the unencumbered land by virtue of its use and squatters rights. Governmental change and politics has often led to conflicting rulings as to the legal rights of the real estate in question. Today, even the local hotel in Andrazza rest on property owned by the families written of herein. Hundreds, if not thousands, of acres of forest were taken or appropriated without any consideration to the rightful owners.

During the later 1800's and into the early 20th century this was not a consideration. There was so much land, lumber and natural resources that no one really cared. Markets were over a hundred miles away with beast of burden driven carts as the only means of transportation. Even with the development of the automobile and railroad it would take years before the roads were improved enough for safe travel. World War I and II would help advance the remote villages, but even this was a slow process due to cost, priorities, graft and politics. The remote mountainous paths were difficult to construct and engineer.

Rivers, mountains, snow, valleys and slides were only a few of the physical challenges that had to be overcome.

Small villages have their own caste system. A hotel or store owner may believe himself above the stonemason or dirt farmer. Certainly the mayor or constable was above the lumberjack. A local priest would place his spiritual holiness far above all. This pecking system however played no role whatsoever in the hearts of the young. As in every corner of the Earth, physical or chemical attractions exceeded every parents warning to 'stick to your own'.

Marshall was a fine strong man in his late teens. His size, looks and cool demeanor made him stand out in any village. His father and grandfather had taught him the family age old skill of cutting stones for mans every use. His strength and keen eye made him a sought after expert in his trade even at a young age. When the fall snows began to fly, he traveled with his father for winter work in the lowlands. This year they went as far as Venizia where their ancestors' names are engraved on buildings the family had built in the fabled city. Even here jobs were scarce and the winters income small. Finally a major commercial job for excellent wages was obtained for both. They worked into May to finish the project. Bonuses were paid to all.

Snow was still in the air as they trekked up the steep winding mountain road. Spring was late. Nearly all of Marshall's earnings were given to his father. He had however purchased some new stylish clothes and factory made boots. Footwear in Andrazza was nearly all homemade or by the local leather smiths. For two days after they returned home, Marshall slept like a log. One must know the brisk crystal clear alpine air before you can miss it. Sleep is in another dimension at 10,000 feet above sea level.

"The   original   family   house"

On day three he awoke late, cleansed, shaved, ate some eggs, drank some fresh goats milk and walked down the long steep slope to the "Little River" to catch some fish. He had missed the fresh mountain trout and he took with him his longest homemade pole and net. Within minutes he had netted a couple large catches for his lunch. Then along the path came two young ladies from the nearby and larger village to the north named Forni de Sopra. Marshall had known both sisters since childhood. They had attended the same school taught by the Catholic nuns. The older sister, Catherine, had always caught his eye. She had the high cheek bones, bronze skin and poise that cannot be taught but are inborn. She had the class of a princess.

"Good morning ladies." He said politely. In these small towns or villages, rudeness or poor behavior was not tolerated. Family feuds could erupt over the slightest of insults. Italian vengeance is a national trait.

"Hello Marshall. How are you?"

"Just fine. Do you wish some fresh trout for lunch?"

Both girls giggled a little.

"We really shouldn't." offered the younger sister who was perhaps 12 or so.

"We do have some fresh bread we could share also."

And so it was a chance meeting of two healthy young beautiful people that would alter their lives and history forever.

Marshall quickly fired a rock grill for the trout while the girls "broke bread". Catherine and Marshalls eyes never left one another. They talked of Venizia, his jobs and clothes. She asked, he answered.

Now Catherine, the 14 year old was from the local bakers' family. Surely not a rich or wealthy clan, but well respected none the less.

Courting would be impossible by the rough crew from Andrazza. They were known to drink excessively, fight and engage in all sorts of distasteful activities. Known as hard workers, their education and social skill left a lot to be desired by the "upper" villagers. Snobs of poverty they were.

After lunch and swearing her sister to secrecy, Catherine made arrangements to meet Marshall the following day at the same time. Night 'dating' was out of the question. Besides there was nowhere to go except the local 'pubs'. This would be foolish for the clans would surely fight over the daughters respect and virginity. Daylight love was in the air and fashionable.

Fourteen was not an exceptionally young age to marry or even have children in Europe at the time. Marshall was not a bad sort, but his family tree allowed a lot of room for disdain by the snobbish. Catherine was young but fully developed. Her mental maturity was far above her age and she knew exactly what she wanted. In this case it was the enormous, good looking, well dressed man she had dreamed of for years. By the second week, Catherine's sister was no longer with her. They had always carted back a fish, fresh berries or greens for the family table. Therefore Catherine's daily ventures in broad daylight seemed innocent enough. Besides the Alps was the safest place on earth.

Marshall's thoughts were on a higher level. Catherine was the Cinderella of his life. He took it very slowly at first, being as naïve as she in the making of love. It was she who had to make the first move. A slight kiss at best. From there on, each days sunlight could not come quickly enough for both to enjoy. Each would fall to sleep reliving that very days newly discovered secrets of the other. Secrets they could never tell but both deep dreamed of in sweat and tears. They both knew they would soon be one and devoted for life. And so it was written. By summer's end Catherine knew she was with child. They married in September and moved into the third floor of Marshall's family stone farm house. The animal odors were gross at first but quickly accepted. Family mannerism, gas passing and heavy alcohol consumption were soon accepted behavior.

Love was splendid but hard. Cooking, cleaning, food preparation for the winter months and child bearing take a lot of energy. Marshall had to continue his winter ventures south for work to help support the family. Marshalls grandfather had passed that following year and Marshall gained the right to a better position both in the house and with the clan. This included his ability to consume large amounts of "Grappa". In spite of all this Marshall worked harder than all others. No job was too small or too hard. He cut timber, plowed land and laid stone. Still he was becoming poorer with each day. Food, clothing and life itself cost more than he could earn working 12 hours a day, seven days a week.

He had to find a way to feed his ever growing family.

Catherine and Marshall had six children in their first eight years of marriage. She was an outcast of her own family in spite of the fact that her two daughters and four sons were the imparity of excellence. She seldom ventured out of Andrazza, instead devoting all of her time to the children and Marshall. As with her husband, she took on every chore from the cleaning the stalls to reaping the crops. Their love and that for their children was what the world was made for. Their love was platinum and family devotion the dream of the saintly. It was bliss that sustained them. Total companionship in which the other each gave 200 percent.

After working and building a new school during their eighth winter, Marshall was offered a job in America laying bricks for a road contractor from Pennsylvania. Skilled masons were few in America and the good ones demanded a fair wage. Transportation and a room would await Marshall on the next sailing. Although his family passage was not included, he packed up the entire family and made imminent plans for the 'chance of a life time'. Marshall had an uncle who had traveled to America and sent flowering letters of America's greatness and wealth. This offer of a job and free passage was a godsend to a poor peasant. Besides, Marshall knew that if he remained in Andrazza it was only a matter of time that a family feud would evolve, Catherine's family continued their public denouncement of Marshall for his inability to support his wife and children

Sooner, rather than later, Marshall would lose his temper and punish the 'dough boys' for their insults.

Chapter II

Voyage to America

So the young couple had agreed, America it would be.

Marshall and Catherine sold nearly every possession they had, including extra clothing and family heirlooms. 'Borrowing' was not in their vocabulary. Furniture Marshall had made, small prizes of jewelry and even personal tools were sold. The economy was in poor shape in Europe. Even these sales produced little more than the boat fare for the family. Still, Marshall gained a job as a laborer on the vessel in order to feed his family until they arrived in the Promised Land. America would answer all their prayers.

It took three days to reach Trieste, their port of debarkation. This ship was far from the gracious passenger vessels seen in pictures. It was in fact a partially converted rusted out freighter. A better term would be rat infested slave boat. However, the tickets were paid and soon they'd be welcomed in America. Their hearts and souls were immune to fear.

Sanitary conditions on the ship were non-existent. Each passenger had to fend for oneself. This was doubly difficult with young children. As a deck hand Marshall had some benefit of taking extra food or blankets to his family. Even this proved of little help. Below deck in the 'hole' the oceans coldness was relentless. Chills to the bone became unbearable pain. Dehydration gave way to serious illness multiplied by lack of medicine or doctors on board. The Greek registered flag ship's captain was nearing his last voyage. His cash bounty had been paid with no sympathy for the passengers.

Each family had been issued two rusty buckets. One to fetch their food and the other with a rope on it, to discharge body waste. The rope allowed the pail to be flushed by hanging it over the side of the boat in calm waters. Marshall was able to procure a second bucket for extra food to feed his family. The food consisted of mostly soups and stale bread.

Living quarters were below deck holds used for shipping bulk fruits or produce. There was no privacy. Some immigrants initially attempted to hang blankets for curtains, but this was quickly realized to be futile due to the wind and the need of blankets to remain warm. By the second day the hole was simply a large steel closet.

Graft was rampant. Deck hands, sailors and even the ships officers would sell anything they could to the severely needy passenger. Even fresh water had its price. Everything and anything was for sale. Experienced sailors knew exactly what food items or essentials brought the highest price once at sea. They also knew the best time to sell their stores. Too soon and the market had yet to peak. Too late the buyers may not have money to pay or need for the product. On this voyage nearly 20% of the passengers would perish, mainly from disease. It was a Spartan trip only for the hearty.

On the best of days, groups of passengers were permitted on top deck for air and exercise. Nothing could be left below deck, even the waste bucket would be stolen by other desperate travelers. The passengers were flirting with death and she would not disappoint them all.

Lucky voyages had good catches at sea. Large fish nets were on board and when available, excess fresh catch was distributed by way of the following day's soup. Even then, those who could pay received the 'best choice'.

The 1918 flu pandemic took somewhere between 50,000,000 and 100,000,000 lives worldwide. Due to mass burials, poor records and the failure of identification, the true number will never be known. Antibiotics were not available and the human immune systems were unable to cope with not only the disease but also the side effects.

The disease was relentless. The Spanish Flu also would take over twenty million (yes, 20,000,000) the coming year. King Cholera still had not been beaten. Typhoid was a killer and the close open quarters gave way for immediate contamination for the sickness to flourish. Within a week the stench below deck was so disgusting the captain ordered everyone on deck and the 'hole' scrubbed. Dozens of bodies were found abandoned by their families or friends. Corpses were tossed overboard for the pleasure of the sharks.

Marshall and Catherine's youngest was a boy named Joseph. He was a strong child with his fathers' size and mothers' beauty. He was the first to contract the sickness and within three days he had passed. Catherine also became ill but with Marshall's feeding, help and liquids, she survived longer than most. Then two days out of New York Catherine passed and was buried without ceremony at sea. Marshall was devastated. The love of his life, his reason for living itself was gone forever. What would he do? He had no money. His family was in no position to care for his five remaining children.

In-laws would now be another problem. They had warned their beautiful innocent daughter about the marriage and damnation that came with it. Certainly it was Marshall's fault and a family feud of deadly proportion would follow.

There was no turning back. America would have to be his salvation.

It was a misty day as they arrived in New York City. Customs and immigration officers stood ready for the nose breaking aromas. All passengers were showered, deloused and reviewed by a nurse for medical problems. Most passengers spoke little more than their native language of Italian, Hungarian, German, Polish or Slavic on this ship. Names were mispronounced and spelled totally incorrect of their origin. This inconsistency continues to this day in census records, birth certificates and immigration documents. Some have estimated that as many as fifty percent of the Ellis Island records are incorrect.

New clothes were issued and all were well fed by the Sisters of Charity and the Red Cross. Marshall had his uncles name and address in Pittsburgh. This was a saving factor for immigration which quickly obtained a train pass for the family; not out of Good Samaritan mind you, but rather the quickest, cheapest method of getting rid of the newly arrived.

Cost was the foremost issue. Processing and retaining the newly arrivals could be a very expensive issue. To clean, feed and quickly send them on their way was the order of the day. A standby train pass would cost next to nothing. Immigration was receiving thousands a day in New York alone. The faster they got rid of their charges the better off for all concerned.

The job promised Marshall had been in Wilkesboro, PA and was no longer available. Some sort of irregularities had eliminated the company and his promised job. Uncle Fabio's Pittsburgh address had qualified him for this pass to the steel city.

Marshall was still in shock from the loss of his wife and youngest son. He was a young man with no formal education, totally unprepared to cope with a tragedy of this magnitude. Still he managed to reach Pittsburgh and find his long lost uncle who now resided in a skid row boarding home. Uncle Fabio was a total drunk. His wife and kids had left him due to his drinking

He worked in a coal mine just outside the city and could have Marshall a job right away. But what about the five children? On Sunday they went together with the five children to the Catholic Church. Uncle Fabio spoke broken (limited) English; but the priest was fluent in Italian. This was a great relief to Marshall who was at a loss for words since he had arrived in America.

The priest was a true saint. He first called the rectory and had the nuns feed and care for the infants while the adults conversed. Rosemary, oldest of the children was only ten, but already a very attractive young lass. Then the priest explained that the church had built the St. Paul's orphanage on nearly 20 acres of bountiful land on the outskirts of Pittsburgh. The orphanage had been started over fifty years heretofore to aid the distressed children of immigrants. The infants would be placed at St. Rita's home till old enough for the orphanage where they would all be fed, educated and cared for till Marshall could care for them himself. Of course he could visit anytime and contribute as he was able to do so. The priest made it very clear that half of Marshall's income should be paid directly to the priest for the children's welfare.

Andrazza never had an orphanage. Families always took care of their own, no matter what. Possibly in Rome or the larger cities children homes existed but this was all totally new to Marshall. What other choice did he have?

There was none. He was in the desert, and this oasis was the only one for hundreds of miles. He signed all guardianship and parental rights to the church. It was the only solution to his problem. That night he and his uncle got drunk on some cheap local hooch before boarding the mines coal train for the ride to their job site. He was hired on the spot at four cents (4) an hour plus a nickel a ton bonus for each coal bin he filled in a day. Each shift was eight hours, but one could work virtually as long as he wished. Company Ltd., trains carried their coal to the mills every hour. There were hundreds, if not thousands, of coal miners on this one job site alone.

Even today in the 21st century, and over 100 years after the fact, more miners die each year in China's mines then the total amount of American lives cost in the Iraqi war. Even with the best equipment, underground labor is the most hazardous of employment. Although statistics are unavailable, and censored by governmental controls other Asian, African and South American countries also lose thousands of lives each year due to mining accidents. Yes, accidents, although many are preventable, cave ins, blast and explosions are devils of the occupation.

Flooding is also a constant fear. Springs, underground rivers and diverted water flows are all causes of mine flooding. If you're 16,000 feet below the earth's surface, and dig beneath a riverbed or into an unknown stream, you're mine will fill up very quickly. The fear of drowning, while trapped in a mine is horrifying.

Mining is a hard dangerous occupation. Knowing how to and when not to cut into a coal vein can be the difference between life and death (literally). The dirty thin air is not only contaminated but combustible. Often, the oxygen is "choked" out, leaving only carbon dioxins in the shaft. This deadly menace was foreseeable by several logical solutions. Caged canaries, dimming lights, and shortness of breath, all gave warnings to the minors. However, if you're a mile deep, with no lights or emergency exit it is a deadly trap for all who fear to tread.

Communication was always a major problem. First and foremost, Marshall spoke no English. It would take years in America for him to become a conversationalist. For now he had to rely on his distant Uncle Fabio to assist him. Secondly, in the early 20th century telecommunications were few and far between. Even more so in the coal mines of Pennsylvania.

Marshall was not alone in his lack of reading, speaking or writing English. Hundreds of thousands of immigrants were welcomed into the New World for their cheap labor. Heavy-handed industrialists well paid lobbyists and corrupt politicians kept entry of limited educated, starving workers a priority in their ongoing quest to line their own pockets. The language barrier made it easy to lie and cheat the new arrivals. No nationality was exempt from the tyranny. Even the immigrants own countrymen would take every available advantage of one another for the almighty dollar, or simply to get ahead.

No one was exempt the embezzlement. The Italians had the Costa Nostra, which would grow into great power and strength. The Irish had their Molly Maguire's, a rough and brutal gang to say the least. The Slavs, Germans and Poles, all had their organizations. Each would take an unfair advantage for their own personal gain. Every dollar was exploited from the miners.

Prejudice raged in the New World. Jokes and sinister cartoons are a matter of media archives. These printed insults gave credibility to the English-speaking nationals to do nearly anything they wished to those lacking the arts of the American predominate language. Teachers, clergy, police and politicians all were with sin. Today's liberals would have been taken to the gallows, alongside the "foreigners". The term, even though the immigrant may have been legal or even nationalized, shows on legal documents, including death certificates and bank statements.

It was a sad day in American history.

The immigrants persecution was relentless. Their dress, food, hygiene and customs were targets for ridicule. They were cheated, stolen from, and constantly harassed by their fellow workers and neighbors alike. Unions were still weak at the time. Those that did exist were corrupt. Taking dues for those services in payoffs from the employees was commonplace.

The real loyalty was in the mines itself. Your life depended on the workers next you. A bond was created linking each man to his entire crew. The majority of coal miners at Marshall's mine were of the Italian descent. Management saw fit to keep Irish laborers on their own crews as Germans on theirs. This was also used as a ploy so that when one ethnic group would complain management would simply infer that the other group could replace the complainers. Even production rates of immigrant groups was used to instigate greater returns. This is accomplished by boasting of one's production to others.

From New York to Ohio and West Virginia coal and iron were being mined at record rates. The Earth's resources were being stripped. Rape of Mother Nature was in full swing. Oil discovery in northwestern Pennsylvania was also removing the liquid gold with no safeguards whatsoever. Contamination by runoffs discharges in negligence went unchecked. Powerful men with big money call all the shots, including contamination, health issues and pollution. A complainant was quickly without a job.

"Mining pick and shovel"

Their efforts went unchallenged by dirty politicians and paid off public servants. Raw sewage, chemicals and steel mill discharges were routinely dumped into the once "most beautiful rivers" in the world. (The first French, who visited the Allegheny and Ohio Valley called it the "most beautiful river."). The greatest names to emerge from the Pittsburgh region were in fact, the very same whom were guilty as sin for their exploitation of mother Earth. For a few dollars more, industrialists' bankers and Congressmen sold America literally 'down the river'. Contaminating the waters as they pocketed millions.

At the turn of the century less than five percent of the miners were unionized in the United States. The united miners union and its efforts for workers rights are legendary. A misconception of mining was that all miners were huge, massive and highly organized. In truth many mines were operated individually and even independently of the larger

41

corporations. This practice of private mining was generally taken over with 'buyouts' as mining became industrialized thus the home owned mines could no longer be competitive with the heavy handed industrialist.

Earliest mines in Europe and even the U.S.A. were often family operated. When a valuable mineral was found on a farm or property the occupants commonly dug the mines, hauled the minerals and prepared the commodity. Preparation for coal included removal of rock or impurities as well as washing and cleaning the product. Many smaller mines had shafts as low as twenty four inches in height. Miners would literally crawl on their hands and knees to reach the coal veins. Small wagons or baskets were pulled and pushed from under the earth to retrieve the production. Women and children were often used for the recovery. Mules, horses and oxen were also used to pull out the earth's riches. Some mules never saw the light of day after being sent underground. Stables, food and water were all kept miles beneath the surface in darkness.

These beasts of burden were common in medium size mines. Their harnesses and straps were hooked to long ropes complimented by pulleys to ease the weight load. A common 'trick' to train the mules was the unreachable carrot six inches in front of the animal. Major problems occurred with the ropes snapping or becoming entangled with rafters and rocks. Mine shafts are seldom dug in straight lines. Deep recovery must not only be dug out but also transported to the surface prior to shipping. Cave 'ins', flooding and gaseous (dust) explosions were common deadly fears of the trade and took (take) more than their fair share of lives.

Railroads were the only reasonable means of transporting the coal to the mills. This allowed the railroads with their federal mandates right of way to lay tracks to the mining locations.

Money follows money and sooner rather than later the railroads became owners of the mines. This was not overlooked by the steel corporations who bought into the rail and mining operations. Multi-board membership was a brotherhood of the industrialist and their cronies.

At the same time the miner was working by production and not by the hour. Some days it would take hours to simply dig out a small wagon of coal from a dying vein. Chalk marks were used to identify a miners 'diggings and coal bins'. These were often changed, stolen or "unaccounted" for prior to pay day. The same miners who risked their lives for pennies were in fact beaten, stolen from and even killed by their employers. Hungry unemployed immigrants were a dime a dozen and employed for even less.

Many mine 'bosses' would issue 'chits' or 'tokens' for each full coal bin produced by the miner. This led to embezzlement and bosses cheating the miner by quick changing, partial payments or even scribbled I.O.U.S. that were later bought back for pennies on the dollar from unknowing immigrants.

Miners were stereotyped as being an uneducated, dirty, filthy lot. Review of miners records shows a different story. In truth over half of those who died in mining disasters had been educated including engineers with graduate degrees. True they were always dirty as they exited the mines but all cleaned, shaved and showered every day. They had to before eating or sleeping side by side with their co-workers. Off duty or holiday miners looked similar to any other blue collar worker; strong, hardy with little fear of anyone or anything. Larger mines had company wash houses with hot showers for the retiring shifts. Smaller mines simply had outdoor hoses and pipes.

These were the Spartans of their era. They gave their all under stressful (shameful) conditions to build Pittsburgh and the U.S. steel industry. Most were paid in company script, a voucher redeemable only at the 'company' store, with prices often twice that of the local merchants where U.S. currency was required. Even the housing was company owned. Rent was deducted even before payday. This colonization left the union and the miners with a distinct disadvantage to the industrialist who quickly became millionaires on the backs of their slaves.

Less than a dozen entities owned over 90 percent of Pittsburgh wealth at the time. This disparity would help the unions to power. Yet this would prove to be a very long and difficult road to travel.

In 1915 the first child labor law, banning the use of anyone under the age of 16 in underground mining in the U.S.A., was passed. This law was as difficult to enforce as the 65 M.P.H. limit is on the interstate. Phony birth certificates, identifications and even passports could (can) be bought cheaply. In remote locations, as well as in 'private' mines, youths as young as 8 to 10 were commonplace prior to 1900.

(Authors note: This writer was employed at age 14 in a steel mill in Pittsburgh.)

Unions and safety issues would come; but very slowly. From 1902 to 1908 alone over 5000 miners were lost to explosions and cave-ins. Steel mills were hardly better.

Strip mining and huge mechanical devices to extract coal were soon perfected for mothers' rape. The multitude of coal mines in the tri-state region were pick and shovel operations. Muscle, sweat and pain brought out the black ore for shipment to the mill and coke ovens. Coal miners were the bottom of the pay scale and social position. Even steel workers and common laborers were considered a step above those who worked beneath the earth. Attempts to organize the miners were difficult. Most miners needed every cent they earned to simply survive. Industrialist such as Andrew Carnegie, a Scottish immigrant himself, employed massive private armies who beat and killed scores of union men. All simply for more profit "on the bottom line."

Unionization was not unique to the United States. Factory workers and miners had been shot by troops in France, England and Germany. In China, Japan and Russia socialism was taking hold over the monarchs' totalitarian rule. British troops numbering over 50,000 strong had to be sent to London to break a national miners' strike. All this upheaval near the turn of the century was both the beginning of true union effectiveness and social reforms for civil rights. Women's rights, race and transparent lives of the financial caste system in America were being scrutinized. Americas freedoms were contagious and being exported throughout the world. Equalities were the new challenge of civilization.

America was on the front burner.

This worldwide movement had little or no effect on Marshall and his thousands of co-workers. Their lack of education, inferior language and limited financial ways of the world made them the most vulnerable of all. They had no money, political clout or means with which to fight the establishment. Only the elected officials had the wealth to become senators and congressmen (or be elected with big money backing). Coal miners had to work simply to eat and stay alive. Still the establishment required the cheap labor supply. Slavery was no longer an option and the destitute Europeans were the next best alternative. Management made every effort to alienate the ethnic groups as well as bring shame upon union organizers. This was accomplished by bringing false charges upon them for everything from embezzlement to child molestation. The mere near arrest of a union member was in itself reason to bring suspicion upon the organizers.

Pittsburgh was the most industrialized city in America. It was growing faster than all others. Its raw materials, rivers and cheap labor made for an unequaled bonanza for investors. Food shortages, lack of medical services and infested housing had no effect on the well to do. The rich got richer and on the backs of the immigrants labor. There was nothing fair or correct of Pittsburgh sins.

It was simply greed.

"Low shaft mine"

"Mule Trains"

Chapter III

A Multitude of Sins

Pittsburgh sins were hardly restricted to the rich. They simply had more time and opportunity for sin. Alcoholism was the commoners' sin of choice. Local "hooch" and homemade rotgut were cheap and readily available. For a couple cents for a bottle of hooch one could hardly walk and even perhaps go blind. For a few cents more legal brew was everywhere even during prohibition. Miners loved to wash the black dust down with a sting. The greater the sting the less the pain. Less pain, less brain.

Miners' safety was another sin. Cave-ins and explosions were a hazard of the trade. Coal workers were required to climb miles deep, dig caves with antiquated tools and no safety standards then bring the ore to the shafts surface literally on their backs. This was not only unsafe but also a death wish. Protective measures were non-existent. Two or three new immigrants stood in line to replace anyone who disputed the horrific conditions. Quitting was not an option. Jobs for unskilled limited linguist were a dead-end.

In spite of all the sinners, violent modern day crimes were non-existent. Home invasions were totally unacceptable and a capital offense, usually by the victim or his neighbors. Kidnapping was also a taboo and very rare except for a shotgun wedding. Of course sin was everywhere. Social changes after the Civil War, the automobile and the soon to come wage differentials all made for easy morals. Folkways and family values were generally left in the old country. One of the few social norms that crossed the great pond was in fact their religious beliefs. Religion was the reason why many made the journey to America in the first place. Some of the very first to arrive were the Catholic priest and missionaries. Others seeking religious freedom were soon to follow in magnitudes.

"The Orphanage"

For thousands, yes thousands, of years men of God have used the cloth as a shield to allow their sinful ways. No man or woman can be so naïve to infer or believe that molestations and rape of children by the clergy has only begun in the last several decades. It has always been there; simply locked in the church closet. Just as gay clergy surely is nothing new. Today's priests simply have a vehicle on which to travel for some sick type of satisfaction. Presently this remains mainly a financial reimbursement for damages although many clergy have now been sent to prison. This is a modern phenomenon. Lawsuits and civil penalties were unheard of 100 or even 50 years ago. Today in many parts of the world the very idea of punishment for a holy man is unheard of. It is this very superior position, untouchable attitude, which allowed the worst of sins for so many centuries. The worst violations of society have gone unpunished for centuries shielded under the auspices of the church. The same church which continues to protect the guilty and not the vulnerable believers.

This will lead to the eventual downfall of the church, unless their leader takes drastic affirmative action.

Turn of the century Pittsburgh was no exception.

St. Paul's Orphanage was originally established with the highest of moral ideals. The first major problem of money was quickly overcome by major contributors who knew that the caring for the children would supply an even larger labor supply for their mills and mines. This also would insure a cheap feminine labor source for menial chores such as housekeeping, cooking and light chores. Child labor laws were non-existent. Payoffs to underpaid cops or agents for years gave orphanages the same sanctuary as the church. They would be taught by the orphanage basic language and most of all how to be obedient. This was the next best alternative to slavery the wealthy had.

By the 1860's the Sisters of Mercy had over 70 girls at their Webster Ave. "home" in Pittsburgh. Then the need to combine the orphanage with the Boy's home in Fennehill was realized. Later yet, in the Crafton/Carnegie area southwest of Pittsburgh, nearly twenty acres was acquired for a new coed orphanage. Huge dormitories, a seminary and school building were built with cheap immigrant and forced child labor which was a requirement of residency. Those who objected to hard labor were beaten and kept unfed. Soon over 1200 orphans resided at St. Paul's. The orphanage retained its status until 1965 when itself destructed and is now utilized as a seminary.

Rosemary was the oldest of Marshall's children. She was now ten years of age and was immediately put to work in the main kitchen of the orphanage. Rose caught on to English with ease. Her culinary skills were quickly appreciated by the watchful nuns and she was transferred to the private kitchen of the clergy. Fresh eggs, vegetables, fruits and meats were enjoyed from local donors and from St. Paul's own gardens where every orphan had to work in the fields. Ethics of production were force fed every inmate. Even the state and federal census referred to the St. Paul residents as "inmates". This designation followed them for life in that they were not legally permitted to leave St. Paul's without written authority which could be withheld until the age of 18. This also generated a cash flow. Several governmental agencies subsidized St. Paul's per pupil, as did donor organizations.

The younger four siblings were housed in the open barracks in double army bunks. Within weeks the youngest, a twin sister to brother Victor, caught ill with the flu and soon passed. Medical care was minimal and preventive drugs costly. One nun who had a few months as a nurse's aide became the "Surgeon of Death" or so the "inmates" called her. It was whispered her examinations were sexual encounters of the first degree where as she digitally penetrated the girls and stroked the boys. Her "inspections" was required and always held in private offices for "security" reasons.

For Roses new job as second chef in the nuns private kitchen sister "Surgeon of Death" insisted on a full body physical examination to insure she carried no diseases.

Make no mistake about it. Even at this pre-teen age Rose stood out in beauty and poise. She was never a show off or boisterous, but rather mature and striking for her age. Her light olive skin was smooth as silk and shined as a harvest moon. A glow was given that would intimidate some while magnetize most. She spoke softly and with purpose always with a smile that was innocent and natural, although surely considered inviting by pedophiles. Her body had just begun to blossom years before most. Rose never attempted to be sexy or inviting. It was simply a fact of life that she could wear a burlap sack and still look like she had just been fitted at Tiffany's. Hers was a beauty inborn, that can never be taught or bought.

Her exam took nearly two hours. Rose certainly was no longer a virgin after this abuse and she bled for two days. Rose now had access to the best foods and took all she could for her three remaining brothers.

At age 11 Rose was coming to full bloom. She was in fact a beautiful looking young lady already. She was now attractive to all the clergy and staff being easy for any eyes. In fact another sister had visited her a couple times for "examinations" and now Father David was making discreet inquiries into the who's and what's of the gorgeous little lass.

Skeptics will cry out "why didn't she complain?" or "call the police?" perhaps "tell the priest". This Monday morning secondary thinking holds no weight. First of all she was a very young, naïve eleven year old; second; who was she to complain to? The other nuns who were in fact their sisters in crime? Third; Rose never knew the police, who or where they were, fourth; Rose spoke very limited English, a distinct disadvantage. Fifth; Rose had been taught that the nuns and priests could do no wrong; sixth, no state or local government oversight existed. (this was the same exact psychotherapy (brain washing) which had allowed the perverted clergy to go unaccountable since the beginning of time.

Rose had nowhere to turn. Her father had only visited once and that was months ago. She thought of running away but to where? Where would she live? How would she eat? Would the boogieman get her? Would God punish her for running away? Surely the nuns would beat, slap and starve her even more than they did now. What could she do?

As a gifted cook, the youngster quickly was the second chef, which saved her from many of the harder chores of floor scrubbing, crop harvesting and disinfections. Simple mistakes such as the coffee too hot or cold and the dropping of food resulted in hard slaps on the face, stomach punches and backside beatings which were common to all "inmates'". The physical punishments began on the very first day and progressively got worse. Speaking Italian was an immediate face slap, perhaps two. Taking food to the dormitory housing received a hard rear paddling. Cussing or not in bed in time resulted in a few good punches or even a day without any food. It seemed the Italians were treated harsher than the rest. Although the majority of the inmates were of Italian origin, many Irish, German, Slavic, Hungarian and even a Frenchman or Greek resided at the orphanage. Nicknamed Sister 'Satan' by the "inmates" she wielded uncanny power. Her word was law. Even the sole resident priest gave her a very wide berth. There were no Orientals, Latinos or Afro-Americans at the orphanage. Recently discovered pictures show a very 'white' student body at the orphanage, which was totally European in origin.

Most students obtained a limited elementary education in formal classrooms taught by the nuns. Problem was the sisters had limited education themselves and less credentials than others to teach the basic three 'R's. Rose got even less due to her kitchen and 'personal' duties. At night she would crawl up into a tight fetal position and cry herself to sleep. She would dream of her Italian Alps, beloved mother and younger siblings. She prayed to God as she had been taught. She knew the sister's molestations were wrong but her young strong golden body had reacted to the pleasant surprise of her pursuers with passionate responses. Once when Rose cried out in pain and another in satisfaction she was beaten to near unconsciousness. This only further confused the already bewildered child.

It was during the end of her eleventh year that she recited the Sisters of Mercy's sins upon her to the priest in the confessional. The priest listened with great interest, asking numerous questions and prying details from the unknowing child. The priest became totally aroused and stimulated by the young girls' narrative. That very night Rose was taken to the rectory. She stayed for nearly two months. Her new job was "clergy special servant".

She was no longer a virgin by any means of the word.

She hurt badly at first. Then the blessed priest convinced her it was in the Lords interest, Gods will and for the good of life itself for Rose to not only submit, but to obey the priest in his every command. She had been selected by the

Almighty to perform Gods will the clergy insisted. God had no mercy.

Rose was cleaning the priest rectory one day (as her new chores called for) when a distinguished man and well dressed woman met with the St. Paul's man of God. It was decided by the priest that Rose would be outsourced as a maid at the home of a wealthy contributor. Here she would have to obey the beck and call of the house "Lord". This was a permanent position and there would be no return. Her good behavior would insure the proper care of her siblings who were being left behind. Should Rose fail in her new duties her younger brothers would receive her punishment and even perhaps be put out into the cold world to fend for themselves. Their young age was no deterrent to the shameless nuns.

The welfare of the children was Roses responsibility. She was the oldest, without parents and thrown into hell without any justification.

Rose certainly had personal worries for her three younger brothers. She also could not have known that the boys were already being abused, both mentally and physically. The infamous hard face slap was used with wooden rulers or a pointing stick when in hand. Many St. Paul inmates took their physical and psychological scars with them to their graves. Due to her good looks, Rose had more heart and soul scars than physical ones. Her brothers and the male populace were not as fortunate. Severe beatings by the nuns were common practice in order to keep the "inmates" in line. They really were not the hardened criminals we relate with prison "inmates". Some were as young as 5 or 6 years of age. Most were extremely shy, of a very informative age and did every chore, duty and task demanded by the despised nuns. The sisters were feared and hated with the same intensity. There were few 'teachers pets' or

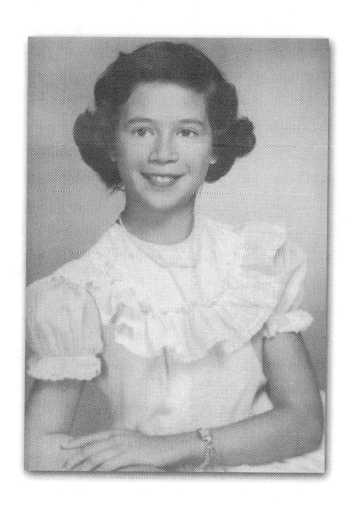

"First Communion dress"

special students. Even the best had to work on the farm and do manual labor three hours for each hour spent in school. This resulted in 12 to 14 hour work days.

Rigid schedules were placed on each student. They were trained to 'Rise with the sun' at the crack of dawn. Ten minutes total bathroom time was allowed in each 25 or 30 person dorm room which had only one toilet and one sink per room. Everyone had to be out of the dorm with beds made, clothes folded in their lockers and the room spotless clean before each meal. Failure to comply was immediate harsh punishment.   In the winter shovels were issued for snow removal. Summer, spring and fall were taken up by every type of farm work. There was also the unloading of food stores from local donations. These were mostly   stale   bread   and   expired   poultry deliveries.

There were exceptions to the six days in hell work week. Sundays were not only for mass and

Sunday school (where catechism was the call). On the Sabbath a family could visit and in the morning everyone was allowed to shower in the jail type facilities. "Inmates" were also required to change clothes and take the past weeks dressing to the laundry themselves. Most had no visitors and recreation time of schoolyard games were played only on a limited basis. Generally this play time was a prop for visitors to see how happy everyone was at St. Paul's.

Morning work periods ranged from two to three hours before they retreated to the dining room for breakfast. The first meal was relatively predictable consisting of toasted stale bread and heated water. Whole bottled milk was only for the clergy. On special winter Sundays huge vats of oatmeal or porridge were served over stale, week old bread. Only when a particularly large donation from a farmer or restaurant was received were the real eggs, fruit or milk seen. This was very rare and only occurred when an inspection occurred or for Easter. The staff ate first with leftovers for the inmates when available. Every bit on every plate had to be eaten without exception by each "inmate". St. Paul's "inmates" were malnourished, skinny and sickly.

Next came mass and then the classroom for another two or three hours. Lunch was simply a piece of fruit on a good day but usually just another stale piece of bread. Perhaps once a week a ½ pint of coffee or a hardened donut would be handed out. Then it was back out to the fields where crops were tended to for another few hours. Prior to dinner a ten minute "potty break" was permitted to clean up before the main meal. This main meal usually included potatoes and vegetables made into a hot watered down stew, which had left over chicken bones or fats added, depending on the donated deliveries. When the orphanage food stores were low portions were cut back. Hot stews and bread crust were the ordinary meal when they were available. After the dinner was prayer hour in the chapel. Finally, as the sun set, they were allowed toilet privileges before lights out. Dorm talking after hours was prohibited. Books were not allowed out of classrooms, leaving only the better students the ability to learn properly.

Rose had three brothers at St. Paul's; James was the oldest and hardly nine months younger than Rose. A year younger was Sam, then Victor. James was both smart and protective. Sam was the toughest and most aggressive. Victor, the youngest was huge for his age, quiet and reserved. They stayed together in everything they did. To fight one you had to fight all three. Sam was dangerous. He would fight at the drop of a penny. There were no Queensberry rules. He would wildly bite, kick or even use a weapon. Victor never would start a fight, but his size scared off most. His brothers the rest. Even the older "inmates" left the brothers to themselves. Rose, with her kitchen job and privileges', constantly took extra food to her brothers. In the chow line she fed them the best with extras. After hours at every opportunity she shared every crumb she could get her hands on. She would however never bring herself to tell of her inner most secrets. The younger brothers had no need to taste her salted pains.

All four did firmly retain a strong family bond. More than kinship, this was a lifelong pledge of life support. Each would have given their all for any of the others. This unity had the Sisters of Mercy take note. Could this family attack or revolt against the nuns authoritative control? The use of capital punishment only went so far. After receiving several face, head and body scars, the brothers' sense of fear had greatly diminished. Other "inmates" also took notice. Apparently the brothers enjoyed fighting and accepted pain as a fact of life. Were they masochist? Or had they simply come to know the meaning of how to cope?

St. Paul's had five main buildings. The large chapel, dormitories, priest rectory, nuns housing and the school/cafeteria. Each was built of stone or brick and huge in size for the era. The chapel was appointed with expensive stained glass, polished wood pews and marble floors. It exists today nearly exactly as it was originally built over a hundred years ago. The multistory dormitory had scores of 25 person rooms and a large cafeteria on the first floor of the school which also had several classrooms. Meals, classes and services, including Mass, were all done by regiments (similar to military protocol). Each building had been constructed with a full basement where oversized coal furnaces were housed. These huge giants had large coal bins besides each furnace where black stones were kept prior to being shoveled into the furnaces doors. Vents regulated the amount of oxygen allowed to 'fire' the coal. The more air the more heat. The more heat the more coal would be needed for fuel.

As with wood, coal has several grades of qualities. Oak burns better than pine and maple over Redwood. Coals better grades were found in and near Pittsburgh under the earth's crust. This best of quality was made into coke and used by the mills in its steel production. This quality was (is) determined by the sulfur and ash content of the producing coal. Several lesser grades were also mined. This was necessary to get to and verify the quality of the vein. Grade two coal ore was also used for steel making, but mostly in smaller specialty mills. Grades 3 and 4 were for heating furnaces and individual uses. Grade 5 was usually tilling left over outside the mine. Grade 5 did in fact contain large amounts of impurities, the exact factor which gave the coal its ratings. (later specifications even had 1 to 50 rates. These impurities included mostly foreign rock and even chemicals.) The more sulfur or ash the lower the value. Impurities would not burn and left a large amount of deposits which had to be removed after the coal burned. The better the grade the higher the quality of the product, as well as a cost factor to simulate. Coal that was not accepted by the mills, overflow and mostly grade 5 tillings was donated to local charities, churches and of course the orphanage. This low quality also gave off a 'rotten egg' smell of raw sulfur.

Pittsburgh winters are long and cold. Even today home and building systems must burn as early as September and run as long as May. The nuns were incredibly thrifty, to say the least. Yet they knew that even the "inmate" must have some heat. Their own quarters, and that of the priest, were always kept incredibly warm. When the coal was delivered it had to be shoveled to the coal slide which fed the bin in each buildings cellar. Each bin had to be correctly packed for maximum storage. Then the coal was continually stored all spring and summer to prepare for the coming winter. After burning, the impurities of rock and ash had to be shoveled out of the furnace, carried out of the cellars and wheel barrowed to their disposal site to the far side of St. Paul's farm where it was spread as fertilizer.

All of the above was labor intense requiring continuous hard work. For these never ending chore the gracious nuns usually selected the oldest and strongest inmates. However, when inmates were determined to be incorrigible or uncontrollable the never ending slave job were given to the worst of the worst.

Of course this death of a job would be bestowed upon the three brothers. But first the evil older sister now in the protection of the priest would have to be somehow removed from her priest protected position. This would take planning and a united effort by the sisterhood, who by now all detested the young slut who shared the clergy's bed as well as enjoying unprecedented special privileges. She was a definite threat not only to the very nuns who had violated her but also to the entire institution.

She had to be excommunicated from the orphanage. Her presence contaminated every sacrament of the holy church. Fornication, statutory rape, child abuse and the misuse of the very commandments to which they had dedicated their lives were all sins that they had to lie about constantly.

Chapter IV

Child Sex Slave

Pittsburgh's religious community was neither exactly close knit nor was it isolated. Certain Christian organizations such as the YMCA, YWCA, The Christian Alliance and other similar groups promoting Christianity, were established institutions. These groups opened lines of communication between Catholics, Protestants, Lutherans and Baptist. Wealthy donors historically contributed their riches to their own denominations. These blessed patrons were well protected and covered by their respective churches or synagogues. The inter-congregational meetings were to share resources such as the Salvation Army or Red Cross. Also much intelligence of social, political and financial matters was passed from one to another when it was perceived to be in the interest of the conveyor.

Prior to St. Paul's purchase of the twenty or minus acres near Chertier, the home had been in Pittsburgh's south side in an area then called Birmingham. A large donor and pillar of Pittsburgh just happened to be in need of a location for his own Boys' Club and youth center. The nuns would receive a large donation for their help in securing the property as well as taking the "inmate" for a sought after job as a maid/Housekeeper at the largest mansion in the city. Personal attributes, activities and persuasions of Rose were also disclosed. She would make a useful 'member' to the millionaires staff for it was told he and or his family had rumors of sinful behaviors. These rumors had surfaced from other employees who somehow had escaped the rich walls of the mansion.

The aristocrats representatives made the agreement with the priest to purchase the south side building, make a good donation and acquire the young maid as a 'gift'.

The price paid to the priest for Rose, was a $20.00 (twenty dollars) 'donation'.

Rose was given no say or even the chance to say goodbye to her brothers. They would learn from other "inmates" days after she had left for a "very good job". The nuns were relieved and the coffers filled with the blood money of a child's well being. She was permitted to take nothing. New clothes and toiletries would be given to her by her new employer. Her father had not been seen in months. His payments to the orphanage were never received. Rose was the eldest yet she had no control or ability to do anything but to accept the inevitable. Her only thought was that "how bad could it be?" Had she had not already visited hell?

The mansion on the north side of Pittsburgh was (is) an international symbol of wealth, power and prestige. The gated entry, flowers, green gardens and huge entry pillars were intimidating to even the wealthy. To Rose this was a palace. Who lived here? Was it the King? The President? Surely she would be safe and sane behind these golden walls. Her plan was to work hard, do every chore, save and then rescue her brothers from the Sisters of Satan.

Gates to hell could not have been more inviting.

In addition to the castle (main house) several other structures were on the estate. These included servants quarters, large green house, carriage house and a guest house. All were of the best construction and finished in elegant grey stone. There was also a large garage for a half dozen wagons or trucks with private apartments above the garages. This building was to the farthest rear of the property.

Below the estate was the point where the Three Rivers meet and the former French Fort Duquesne once stood.

Streets in Pittsburgh were beginning to be paved. The downtown and north side, homes of the well-to-do, came first. Asphalt and cement highways with reinforced iron had not made their debut as of yet. Customary were the brick or cobblestone streets. Hundreds of transporters and laborers would feed the masons who would lay the stones on well prepared level formations. Later many of these brick roads would be asphalt covered. Many, untouched, remain to this day, a hundred years thereafter. Marshall was gifted as a stone mason and when the mines were slow, unions on strike or unable to work beneath the ground, he found employment laying the brick streets of Pittsburgh. As a tribute to the era, as well as a speed and safety measure, cobblestone streets are twenty first century clique architecture and used in many old town areas such as Sacramento, San Antonio and Savanna.

All the streets around the mansion were cobblestone or brick. City workers cleaned, swept and landscaped the adjacent streets daily.

On her arrival, Rose was taken to the servant's quarters where she 'shared' a room with five other maids and cooks. They had a private bath and private gleaming wooden "wardrobes" for their cloths and uniforms. The other girls were mostly in their early twenties except for a seventeen year old Irish girl who had recently fallen out of favor with the host family. The girls name was Ann. The girls immediately bonded as 'semi' outcast of the nearly entire Protestant, German/Austrian/Bavarian staff. Ann was attractive and not at all intimidated by Rose with her good looks or her youth. Ann never confided as to why she had lost her private apartment or all the hatred of the other servants. The half dozen male employees kept their distance from the female staff. Even a passive relationship would be reason for immediate dismissal.

Four of the males lived in the men's room which also had its own bath. One male, the head chef, lived off the estate with his wife and two children. The landlord had brought him over from Vienna where his culinary skills were a national treasure. The final, most important of all was the butler. This giant of a man was the confidant, manager and boss of the employees. He could fire, beat or have jailed anyone he wanted. The head of the house allowed the butler full control of his subjects. A hard slap, punch or kick was not an uncommon to combat bad behavior or poor performance.

The carriage house to the front of the house was actually the guard's house manned by the Pinkerton Security. The Pinkertons had long established a hard fast, vigilante type of private police in service for the rich. Political power from both the rich clients and Pinkerton himself allowed the 'private police' a lot of authority which was generally approved of by the local authorities. Large sums of money at the federal, state and local level paid the police chiefs, district attorney and the local captains to back not only the Pinkertons in all their ventures but also to protect the capitalist and America's most wealthy. A short time earlier steel workers had gone on strike at Carnegies Homestead Mill. Thousands stood on picket lines for fair wages and safe working conditions. Pinkertons, with the support of the Pittsburgh Police, broke the back of the strike. Scores of strikers were killed and Carnegie, the Pinkertons and the Pittsburgh Police got away with murder. Even the local priest condemned the union strikers saying it was not in Gods way or the good of the church for workers to dissent. (They must have forgot that Jesus was a dissentor!) Decades later the nuns and priest would begin to take a more liberal role in political matters. All in the name of God.

One hundred years ago the education, training and governmental constraints upon the Catholic Church in particular and religious institutions in general was, to say the very least, uncontrolled. The separation of Church and government left a black hole of unanswered questions. Curriculum, number of school days and hours were all decided by local churches. St. Paul's orphanage is an excellent example. At this time not one sister, not one nun, not one teacher at the facility had a college degree or teachers credential. Not one. The existence of any psychologist, social worker or psychiatrist was also lost in the black hole. The merciful nuns did cry "does not our years of teaching make us qualified?" "Does not our continual work with the "inmates" make us experts?" To which one must respond, "Drowning does not make one a swimmer"; to beat young children into submission makes one not a psychologist or specialist, but rather instead a sadistic monster in need of help herself. If so, were the priest who were molesting children for hundreds of years experts in pedophilia?

Even the terminology used at St. Paul's ("inmate") insinuates a prison or confinement. Hospitals have patients, not inmates unless it's a psychiatric ward. As students without parents they were orphans and disadvantaged. Never "inmates". As wards of the state, did not the church, Catholic hierarchy and Sisters of Mercy have an obligation for the welfare of the children? We have come a long way in the backs of these enslaved. Today's society would not allow such abuse. Yet then not only were the politicians on the take but this filtered all the way down to the cop on the block.

Not all nuns were sadists. However, strictly enforced punishment is contagious. This acceptable contagious misbehavior was equally true by passive priests, fat politicians and underpaid police. As with the clergy who had been molested in their own seminaries, the bad apple laid many seeds. This misbehavior certainly was never isolated to Catholicism. It was simply even more unpleasant due to the related religious over-tones. The problem that these sick perverts had on the "inmates" was a very deep, lifelong scar. Inhibitions were exaggerated at a formative time. Instead of maturity the "inmates" lost total self confidence. The inability, lack of training and little or no education of the keepers, gave no direction, morals or goals to the "inmates". The Sisters of Mercy in no way were typical. They were simply overwhelmed with little or no way to control hundreds of poor, low, rebellious class "inmates". (A good start might have been to stop calling them "inmates".)

Rose was no longer called an "inmate" but rather a "maid in training." Servant's wages were non-existent to "maids in training". They ate in their own "servants" kitchen which separated the female and males rooms. The food was quite good especially compared to the orphanage. Meals were quick and simple. The butler insured every hour was time well spent for the estate. The uniforms were white shirts and black skirts with black shoes. Uniforms always had to be clean and ironed, "cleanliness was next to Godliness". No stone or rug was left unturned. Butler, as the staff supervisor, constantly inspected kitchens, bathrooms, halls and rooms for the slightest of sins. He also carried a stick similar to a walking cane but made of hard handcrafted hickory. His temperament was known to strike an offender on the hand for eating improperly, speaking out of turn to the backside or even on the chest which was difficult for the ladies to defend. Butler lived in one of the upper rear apartments above the garages. There were three units there, each with their own bath, small kitchen, large brass bed, radio and carpets.

His dedication to the master of the house was uncompromised and unrelenting.

Rose, having just turned 12, surely didn't want Butler's stick to cross her body. Her English had improved well although she remained a quiet person. She slept very well the first night and awakened at the crack of dawn. She loved her new clothes and took a scissors and needle to them before the others saw the sun shine. She was proud of her well fitting blouse that she had tapered, stitched and pressed the creases with care. Having had a year of maturing allowed her to look far more older than her age. She was nearly 5'2", 100 pounds of excellent proportions and wavy harvest brown hair now down past her shoulders. Butler demanded her to wear her hair above the neck in a bun.

The wealthy owner and his family were presently home. This was not always the case. They had summer homes in the mountains and at the ocean as well as trips to colleges, New York, Washington and even Europe. This allowed the staff certain free time from duties but not a lot. Private schools and tutors educated the host family while the parents participated in every social function available. River cruises, picnics, orchestras, plays and sports events were always completed with a large dance or ball. The best of Pittsburgh attended. Non attendance was considered a mortal sin in the eyes of Pittsburgh's society. Not to attend was dishonorable and inexcusable in the eyes of social elite. Extra part time staffers were commissioned for each affair. Gay affairs they were. Money was no object. The best of food and spirits flowed as do the rivers they overlooked.

Rose had been sold into and blessed upon by one of the wealthiest clans of Pittsburgh's finest.

On the Friday of her very first work week, Rose was on kitchen duty serving for the main house. Her best outfit had been inspected as were her fingernails, hands and hair for cleanliness. Even her new shoes were shined. Her own tailored uniforms fit as a model.

Looks, chemistry, even infatuations, have been written about by philosophers since the beginning of time. Basic animal instinct to mate is often overcome by social norms and folkways. Yet from holy men and women to the highest of positions (including presidents) people leave their morals in the closet when the bolt of sexual attraction strikes them. As most become more mature with families or responsibilities, the morals become more and more important. Out of respect for family most brush aside the moments charge. This desire is often more acute in the most powerful of men commonly called the alpha male. Their unrestrained motivation to succeed, which made them successful in the first place, drives them to obtain their every wish. Here at this family dinner the master of the house couldn't keep his eyes off this gorgeous little creature helping to serve his dinner. The entire meal was never tasted. Salt was in his veins. Sugar in his loins. Oh lord she was so beautiful. So desirable. So innocent. He would gladly give $1,000,000 for her. Yet he had her right here. Had not his wife caught him with Ann only two weeks here to fore, he would have taken this child to his private office for consultation. He had to be careful. His very eyes told his wife, the mother of his children, of his furtive desires.

Since Adam and Eve the male vs. female chemistry has been the subject of controversy. Every psychologist, expert and talk show host has his or her own opinion as to who's the smarter, stronger or better fit to lead. There can be no argument that the physical differences have a direct effect on each mental set as well as decision making. There are no hard and set laws. Each and every species is unique to that particular set of circumstances.

Wealth, strength and fame change the equation significantly.

Men say all women are strange animals. The truth is men are equally or even more so 'strange'. It was not only his physically challenged or twelfth hour laborer you must hear. Alpha men with great financial conquest, political power and social standing, all have drives equal to and usually greater than the rest. The master felt himself becoming aroused, fuzzy and hot, for the child serving his family dinner. There was light sweat on his brow and the stiffness his wife no longer craved. Intellects often say they are above this but in fact his urge is what has made the world go round for 20,000 years.

Dinner was not even finished when instructed Butler to have his coffee served in the 'Library'. Few were allowed in the privacy of his library. It was (is) a huge room with law books and encyclopedia from around the world. Natural polished solid oak paneled walls and shelves overlooked the massive stone fireplace which grew to the ceiling. Hardwood parcay floors were highlighted by five Persian spun area rugs. Deep mahogany leather chairs and a thick cushioned couch were spaciously positioned. It was his room and his alone. Company acquisitions, investment and financial matters were often decided here. Notes on cost, debits or credit, were abundant on his gigantic Black Maple desk. This was in fact his war room. The library had three exits. In addition to the main double door there was also the side door to the main kitchen area plus one glass French door to the private garden.

As always it was Butler who brought a pot of coffee, European gold rimmed cups and all the compliments to his master on a large polished true silver tray.

His perverted thoughts for the child were far reaching. He fantasized of numerous sexual encounters with him in total control of the child. He would demand she perform, submit and engage in whatever his warped mind decided. She would obey completely his word as law.

Now this very rich man was not unlike most. He put each foot in each pant leg, brushed his teeth and showered as we all do. True the pants were tailored silk, the teeth well cared for by the finest dentist in the world and the shower or tub was the size of most people's living room. Still he was not a bad man. He was a Christian, (at least in spirit, if not soul) supporting the church and several social organizations. Psychologists would analyze this in part from his hard work and long hours. This also eliminated his time for the family. The man participated with vigor in all the top society functions. Money certainly was no object.

In spite of all this, he was a sick pervert who believed himself above the law.

He awakened early the following morning, having a light breakfast before fulfilling his daily corporate duties in the library. Several days a week he would travel the few blocks to the plant but this was not necessary every day. The plant operated with top notch conscientious managers, practically running itself. His labor, supplies and sales ran like a Swiss clock. Accounts, project managers and supervisors supplied the data but the important decisions were his to make, which he did well.

He now had the money, position and power to do nearly anything he wanted to do. Sex with young girls was indeed his chosen poison.

Chapter V

With Child

Rose and her few belongings had been moved into the far corner studio apartment above the four car garage. Butler lived in the first unit. A second unit was kept for special guests or needs and the third was the special "playpen". The staff and Pinkertons all knew this apartment well. It was suspected, but never confirmed, that even the masters wife knew but never so acknowledged. The staff joked it was simply his hobby and that he enjoyed playing with "toys". The more upright and religious employees simply turned a deaf ear in shame.

Ann was both hurt and relieved. She had lost her ever so comfortable private room yet on the other hand she no longer had to 'service' the master. He was often rough and had done several hurtful actions to her including sodomy. She had hurt and cried out in pain which only seemed to arouse the master even more. He certainly was not a large, endowed person. She had had not only her own room for the past year but also nearly no chores except as a pleasure toy. Ann knew, beyond any reasonable doubt, what Rose was in for. The pain of her life was about to transfer onto the poor newcomer. There would be no mercy.

No staff member would dare complain. Any protest at all would result in immediate termination or perhaps worse. All Butler had to do was to charge the underling with theft and a year or two in jail was sure to follow. Good jobs were tough to come by and this was the best pay in the finest estate in the entire city. Everyone looked the other way in fear of reprisals.

Of course the staff, and even the master himself, had no way of knowing that the beautiful little lady had been molested, abused and raped by the chosen ones of God for the past year. She had been taught (told) to not only enjoy sex but also to never complain. Rose had simply enjoyed sex too much which was a threat to the nuns and their own security. She was far too young and naïve to believe she could be a threat to anyone. She wished no one harm, had no ambitions and hardly understood the pecking order theory. In truth she had a wonderful happy heart and soul. Nice people with good intentions had no chance of survival when tossed in the lion's den. Wolves eat sheep.

Butler had seen Rose at the servants breakfast. He had discretely addressed her, out of ear shot of the staff that some new clothing for her was in the closet of her new room. After eating she was to return to the room, shower and dress in the new clothes. Then she would

104

wait there until the master of the house came to visit her.

"Do you clearly understand my instructions?"

"Yes sir."

"Any questions?"

"Yes sir."

"What?"

"How long do I wait?"

"A week or two if I tell you. You better get it straight right now that this is your only sanctuary in the world. We feed, clothe and take care of all your needs. You must only do everything, and I mean everything, you're told. Understand?"

"Yes sir."

"And shampoo your hair also. You'll love the coconut fragrance. It's in the shower for you with the French beauty soap."

"Yes sir."

"Ok, Ok, off with your child. Now."

Rose ran to the back room that was now her own. She had never had her own room and this one was beautiful. The new clothes certainly were not working clothes. The very short pleated skirt was more of a school girls uniform and the white blouse was silk with matching underwear. Butler hadn't lied. The shampoo was a rare treat.. The quality was nearly good enough to eat. Even the soft 'Paris' soap made her feel like a woman. Her silky lightly waved natural hair dried quickly as she brushed it out. Even the brushes and mirrors were top of the line. Ole butthead did his job well.

She had waited over two hours when the door opened and in came her master; her owner, her keeper, her pursuer, her molester, her rapist. No matter how willing, there is no way any 12 year old has the ability to consent to intercourse. This had no impact on the masters predetermined goal. He was used to having his way. His company, the money and connections rendered him above the law. He could, and did, nearly anything he wanted. In his own mind he rationalized he was doing the poor immigrant a favor. He gave her shelter and would teach her the arts of love making. Was he not doing her a favor? She was the lucky one. In his own mind, she was the chosen one.

His eyes were about to be reopened. Very wide.

Inside the room he immediately put his arms around the young girl. Both hands searched every inch of her body. First outside her sweet smelling clothing and then inside.

However he was stunned that not only did Rose fail to resist but rather Rose became the aggressor. How could this child know so much? At his insistence they were unclothed and in bed in short order. She knew exactly where and how to touch him. How to use her body and whimper like a pet. The pleasure was so great they were at it a second time a half hour later. Then after showering together a third, fourth and finally just before dinner a fifth. He was exhausted but went to the head of the family dinner table with a very broad smile on his face. Every muscle in his body was relaxed. His blood pressure was the lowest in years. She may have unknowingly saved his life. All the stress of high finance and success were diminished by raw sex. And this was by far the greatest sex he had ever experienced. His wife knew her husband's mannerisms. She knew immediately what had transpired.

Historically he had never conversed or befriended his conquest. They were generally very young, inexperienced mostly virgins of poor social status. This made his subjects not only vulnerable but also at a distinct disadvantage to ever complain or demand compensation. Most would last only a few months. Their services were demanded only once or twice a week at most. They were however always on "call". Few if any other duties were assigned to the chosen one. They were in fact adolescent sex slaves.

Ann had been an exception to the general rule. As a young teen she was not only in excellent physical condition but also a very pretty little thing. Butler knew never to recruit large or tall servants who were unqualified candidates for employment at the mansion. Only the very young and petite were selected. The pool of applicants was enormous. For every job there were 100 applicants. Not only was the house the most prestigious but having worked there opened the door to any employer in the city.

The definition for pedophilia has changed over the past 100 years and continues to change in countries throughout the world. Girls as young as ten continue to have children in third world countries. In certain southern states fourteen had been the legal age of consent. With parents permission age was never a factor in most states pre WWII. Today a pedophile is still the adult who takes unfair sexual advantages of his/her underage prey. Yes, in recent years the female adult has now become the prosecuted predator. This was unheard of years gone by. Predator and prey are accurate terminology. As with one animal stalking another for a kill, there is little difference here. Instead of stalking or enticing his victim this wealthy, well-mannered capitalist simply bought his subjects.

The infatuation was beyond the master's control. Rose totally consumed his every thought. He was visiting her several times a day each with multiple sessions. He quickly scheduled a family vacation to the coast. Having no intent of ever going, an excuse was made at the last moment for him to stay at home due to work. His wife knew the truth. Now he could sleep day and night with his cherished child toy.

By the second month they had had sex every single day. Often several times each day. She had no other chores. Butler furnished the best of foods to the room as well as some of the finest clothes. She sensed something was wrong when her monthly had not come. She felt it was normal due to the continuous sex. No one had ever explained about protection, the reproductive systems, having a child or even the correct hygienic procedures. At less than 100 pounds her small tight stomach soon showed that the seed had indeed been planted. At five months the masters finest toy would have to be removed from the house. This scandal would be blamed on another. Perhaps an employee or even a Pinkerton. It was their duty to confess to such a sick crime. Perjury was part of their obligation.

But where would they put her? The orphanage was out of the equation. Besides the "Merciless" sisters would no doubt demand large sums of money to stay quiet. Even then there were no guarantees. It was the ever so resourceful Butler who suggested a meeting with the local police captain, the Pinkerton manager, his master and Butler beset to find a solution to the problem.

The meeting was set for the very next night.

Captain McNaulty was a large hard self made Irish immigrant. Have risen from the streets he had no doubt who buttered his bread or fed his family. The law protected the rich and McNaulty was the law. The north side and Troy Hill were his precinct. He made the calls and kept the peace. His word was gold. No one crossed a police captain and got away with it, except perhaps his chief or the ultra very rich. He was a dedicated and decorated cop who had come up through the ranks by hard work and blind loyalty.

David Moore was an educated man from New York. His dad was a carpenter and his mother a seamstress. At college he had been recruited by the Pinkertons who trained him as they wished. As a football star and athlete he was an excellent candidate. This grooming had taken over 10 years. This position was a career step and he knew he would do whatever that was required of him. Pinkertons were known for their violence and own style of justice which was heavily handed out with little or no recourse by the adversary. Pinkerton had gotten away with murder at the Homestead steel mill. This was a piece of cake.

They met in the library. Butler had the top shelf liquors and wines available to which the guest gladly enjoyed.

"Well gentlemen, you know my problem? Any suggestions."

"There is a new unwed mother's home on the south side." Captain McNaulty stated.

"Who runs it?"

"Believe it's the Catholic church nuns I'm told."

"That's out; can't trust them."

"Ship her back to the old country." Came Moore.

:"No, her family would soon raise stink."

After a short pause, it was Moore who stunned the other three.

"She could have an accident and fall into the river. It is high this time of the year. Happens all the time. She may not be found until she reaches Ohio."

They were all very quiet.

Captain McNaulty broke the silence.

"That's a bit overkill for a solution. The crime, disappearance of a child. Just don't make sense to me."

"It's my problem and it will be my solution. But I agree. She does not deserve that."

"My staff tells me her dads a coal miner." Captain McNaulty said.

"That's true." Came Butler.

"New boarding homes are being built next to the entrances to the mines. Let's get her dad a small promotion, make her the boarding house maid and ship her out of town with her old man."

"And if she tells her old man who the father is? What then?" Butler asked.

"If he's smart he'll enjoy his new job. If not he may disbelieve her anyway. What's he to do? No lawyer or cop will take any action in this town. Even her word would be in question. Who would believe a 12 year old wop?"

"Do we know of any new miners houses?"

"Yes sir. One's at mine #3 in Castle Shannon just south of us. It's up and ready to open. The other I checked on is New Bethlehem say 70 miles north of us. That will be completed next week and ready for boarding. It's a small remote town, should be a perfect put away."

They all knew that Castle Shannon was a large and growing mine hardly five miles cross the Monongahela. This huge coal mine included several large shafts and numerous dwellings to house the miners. The mines sat (sits) between three large "coal mountains" along Saw Mill Run and Pittsburgh's southern hills. Major problems of the close proximity and access to union organizers or agitators gave bad grades to this high producing facility. The town of Castle Shannon was actually built on top of the mine shafts.

The Pittsburgh/West Virginia railroads and later the Pittsburgh, Castle Shannon and Washington ran narrow gauge 40 inch wide rails to Castle Shannon for its coal. These lines connected the Mt. Washington mines with Castle Shannon and Pittsburgh's riverside mills. Mt. Washington, formerly known as "Coal Hill", had several shafts but was small in comparison to the Castle Shannon and its neighboring Brookline digs.

Odds are that the majority of homes built in these mining districts still today are under mined by the coal shafts of yesteryear.

"It's settled then." Came the master's call, "New Bethlehem's far enough away. Perhaps we'll never hear from them again. Butler you take care of all the arrangements. Thank you gentlemen. Butler has an envelope for each of your families."

Rose never knew how close she had come to taking a late night swim in the Ohio River. A swim which would have been difficult with large rocks tied to both her legs and hands tied behind her back. She was permitted to take all the clothing given to her and personal items with her.

It was this day that she stood at the window watching the masons laying the new cobblestone road behind the masters garage. Her thoughts were of the very hard work, low pay and conditions of the working class when compared to the rich. Was it fair? She had touched the sleeve of the very upper class and didn't like what she saw.

She didn't like it one bit.

Chapter VI

The Great Escape

While Rose was "sporting" with her master, her three brothers were plotting their escape from hell. With their sisters departure from the orphanage came more beatings from the nuns without mercy. Two of the nuns wore belts with large cowboy type buckles. These were used to beat and punish those who did not comply with their blessed command. Verbal and mental scoldings were reinforced with harsh whippings. The belt buckle often left welts and scars for life. All three of the brothers had numerous scars on their heads, hands and backsides all caused by the "Sisters of Mercy".

The amount of pain inflicted upon the "inmates" is beyond authored explanation. Prison "inmates" are treated far better than the St. Paul's orphans. Nuns believed their physical

"Under mining the city"

abuse was their God given right. Punishment for even minor infractions was instantaneous and harsh. Broken ribs, arms and legs went untreated. Deep gashes received iodine instead of stitches and antibiotics. The Sisters of Mercy could do no wrong. They were untrained, uncontrolled and mismanaged. Crimes of St. Paul's should have resulted in felony convictions. Yet local officials looked the other way. Who else could or would care for the unwanted children? "Not I." Said the politicians, taxpayers or even Gods own clergy.

Hundreds of children, "inmates", could not be cared for, housed, fed or educated by the existing infrastructure. Money was being invested in roads and rails for Pittsburgh's industrialization. Nothing was available for the indigent youths of America. Nothing that is except brutal beating, poor food and the mental deprivation of thousands. Medical treatment was non-existent,

"Bless you father for you have sinned."

The brothers plot was simple enough. They would first acquire by theft all they could. Items would be kept in the darkest hole of the coal bins where they were forced to work. No one ever came down into the damp cold cellars. A partially ripped discarded army duffle bag was appropriated to keep their prizes. Anything an inmate might misplace, from their shoes to a towel, was taken. Nothing was taken from their own dorm till the final day. An extra blanket left hanging here or a pair of socks there were subject to confiscation. Food was also on the hit list. At first they targeted canned goods and non-perishables that they could steal from the kitchen. Nuns cigarettes (yes, they smoked!), loose change and even one of the dress belts was acquired. It was a given, if they got caught they'd be scarred from head to toe with the worst beating imaginable.

For three days prior to "E" day, they took all the bread and fruit they could stuff in their pants. Every institution has snitches. Some are called whistle blowers, rats, tattle tales or loose lips. But a snitch is a snitch, whatever you might call him. Nearly everyone knew who the snitches were. A pre-emptive strike was executed. The brothers agreed that they must silence the snitches by use of physical fear. Three of the older most feared snitches were separately and secretly ambushed by the brothers. They beat one in the lavatory late at night, another remotely on the farm and a third in the rear of the church. They had stalked each snitch lying as a gang to strike their target. These were savage gang type beatings. Bones were broken and blood left to flow. Each was told the beatings would be permanent if they revealed anything concerning the brothers. If any discipline of any type whatsoever came back to the brothers, the beating would become even worse.

Word spreads quickly in close knit housing. Everyone knew or had a good idea of what had taken place. Bullies and snitches alike were now confronted with a younger but fearful threat. "Three on one is not much fun." A wide path to walk was allowed the outcast family. They then put the strong arm on inmates who had Sunday visitors. Money, gifts and even personal tokens were taken from their rightful owner in fear of retaliation and a good beating by the three crazed brothers far outweighed the value of the lost items. Never a word or complaint was filed.

Exiting the walled and lock gated orphanage was simple enough. Just south of the main gate the large stone wall became a six foot cyclone fence. Behind one tree the fence had a small hole made by a tractor coming too close. The boys had spent hours enlarging the hole which could now be easily crawled through. Jimmie, the oldest and wisest, made most of the decisions. His planning was excellent.

On the night of the great escape they waited two hours after the lights were out. They had all slept several hours that day on their coal bin time, deep in the cellars darkness. Their bounty was readied. It would take two to carry the heavy duffle bag, so they decided to take the coal bins wheelbarrow with them. As they left their dormitory each took a second pair of shoes from preselected roommates. Each pair had been well stalked out for size and condition. They also took all their own clothing, heavy coats as well as their entire bedding. They had no intent to ever return.

The three pre-teens were a sight to behold. Pushing a cart covered by an old army blanket, themselves in rags would make a poster picture for all the charities soliciting your dollar. Here it was in the most industrialized city in the world with poverty walking the very same streets that the wealthy had paved for themselves in gold!

Pittsburgh had had several major floods and many more of lesser devastation. Even in recent years despite dams, locks and controls, the city continues to flood, especially at the confluence of the Allegheny and Monongahela. When the Ohio River was (is) swollen the backup naturally flushes into the 'Burg'. One, in particular that occurred in 1907 was a 100 year flood of Biblical proportions. Constant rains over several weeks had pushed debris and garbage for hundreds of miles. The uncontrolled water had no choice but to settle where the rivers met. Even the original builders of Fort Duquesne and its successor by combat, Fort Pitt had flooding problems. After the 1907 flood a major water control system was built stretching as far north as Clarion County and eastward to New York. Dams were constructed strategically for the regional protection. It is ironic that the same who raped Mother Nature then attempted (unsuccessfully) to control her?

To this very day, the Point, downtown Pittsburgh and several precincts, remain subject to seasonal flooding.

On this day it was late summer and still dry. The brothers were blessed with good weather and a full moon.

They had sneaked out this exit a dozen times over the past two weeks. A farmer took his crops to the city's early market where restaurants and stores bought wholesale produce. He had agreed to give them a ride into the city for their guarantee to help unload his heavy cart. It was a fine exchange for both. Today's load was especially heavy. The farmer had loaded everything and two horses strained to pull them to market.

Pittsburgh farmers market was an institution unto itself. Prior to Fort Pitt being built, the local production was taken to the rivers banks for sale and trade. Indians had traded beaver pelts on the same rivers edge long before the white man's migration. Even then the area was subject to flooding and not prime for development.

Wagon trucks and even boats would bring their wares to barter on this centralized unbuildable real estate. Large loads, as with the one the boys were riding, were unloaded so buyers could easily see, sample and make a bid. Sales were brisk and plentiful.

They were among the first to arrive to the river side site of the market. Their driver selected the best of locations. He had been coming here for years and knew the weekly protocol. It was first come first to select the best location. The brothers were the best of workers. This was child's play compared to shoveling coal at the orphanage. They carefully unloaded the wagon stacking each crate neatly in a categorized order. An apple was given to each brother for his work. As the red sun rose above the stacks of smoking mills the market came to life with buyers from every walk of life. These were nicely dressed, but not overdone, food service people from every corner of the city. Sales went quickly. Restaurants, sidewalk vendors, local produce wagons and grocers came in large numbers. Buyers knew their needs and sellers their product. The boys had nowhere else to go so they remained to watch, and learn. After walking around watching the 'oh so many' vendors, they sat in the now empty wagon and watched the farmer sell everything he had except a half crate of overripe green peppers.

"You boys are good workers. Tell you what. Yez load them empty crates back on my wagon you can have the ½ crate of peppers for free."

"Yes sir, thanks boss!" Jimmie shot back.

After loaded, the farmer continued:

"If you're all here next week, I'll do you even better."

131

"Oh we'll be right here."   As they waved goodbye.

After loading their new crate into the wheelbarrow they once again walked the market place.   All sorts of materials were discarded or left behind.   Broken crates, over and under ripened fruits and vegetables and even a wagon with a broken axle from being overloaded, had been left behind.   In all they accumulated two dozen broken crates, mostly with leftovers in them.   Over the years unwanted materials had been routinely thrown in the river or simply left to the high waters which carried them down river.   Not unlike the great industrialist, thought was never given to those down river.

Jimmie spoke first as the last wagon departed.

"Hey, let's drag that broken wagon up here to the best spot."

With that, the three boys pushed and pulled the old wooden wreck to the high spot of the market. This was indeed the prized, finest location in the market.

"Let's stack the crates up around us and maybe build a fire in that old metal drum left over there."

"We can't eat all this stuff. Should we toss it in the river?"

"Hell no! We'll wheelbarrow it around town and sell it off."

The three brothers had never been exposed to the big city. Somehow they fit right in. Sidewalk cafes, mill workers coming home from work and even a small corner market bought nearly all the boys could carry. Soon nearly three dollars in change was in their pockets. Homelessness was not an issue in Pittsburgh at this time. Everyone had a job. As in the old country every family took care of their own, everyone had a roof. Most were hard laborers in mills and mines. Perhaps it didn't pay much, but it was a job.

Pay was low, very low. Yet so were the cost of food and housing. Flop house beds could be had for a couple of dollars a month. Hamburgers or foot longs five cents. A half decent home could be purchased for a few thousand dollars. Produce, fruits and market products were also unbelievably inexpensive. Even today, Pittsburgh is one of the most affordable cities in the U.S. in which to live. Constant production of steel products gave a boost to every aspect of the city. Bricks were produced at a fraction of a cent each due to the local raw materials being readily available. Inexpensive construction gave rise to thousands of multistory brick row home, most of which remain standing today.

The streets and neighborhoods were rough. Bullies, punks and perverts were common. The brothers always together and always as one, were never intimidated. Hoodlums had to beat all three before beating one. At any sign of trouble they operated as a military unit. Sticks, bricks and kicks were equalizers which they never hesitated to use. They had learned pain in the orphanage and knew how to handle it. Power of unity from pledging the flag to Semper Fi are the "backbone of the country" as well success! The three Italian boys may have drawn attention had they been active for a longer period of time. For the short haul, they were generally left alone, as you do a sleeping dog.

That first week the brothers had acquired over three more dollars from sales of their leftovers. The following week they awaited their friend and after having saved his favorite space, again unloaded his wagon. Then they ran from vendor to vendor helping set up their day's goods. Some would toss them an Indian Nickel or a few cents but all gave them a taste of their home grown. Each vendor was proud of what he had produced and to see the boys' eyes light up was true exhibit of their pride. Climatic conditions, rich soil, ample rain and good farming continued to produce fine crops in this region.

Due to a very light early fall rain and being the end of the month, sales were slower than the previous week. Many partial crates of unripe goods were spilled out or left behind by the vendors who were mostly leaving early. This coupled with the unsold over ripe produce gave the brothers a full wagon of sellable items. The vendors all knew they no longer had to dump the leftovers in the river, but instead gave them to the "Three Italian guys". This was also less work and easier for each vendor. They knew their spaces would be clean the following week. The brothers used the empty crates they had to collect their prizes then wheelbarrow them back to the inoperative wagon which by now was their home.

While on their neighborhood tracks they had come to quickly know the turf. Trash was generally put out on Thursday for pickup. Pieces of metal, plastic and plywood were stacked on the wheelbarrow then taken back to the wagon where a shack was built. And indeed a shack it was. Built by children from tossed out junk it didn't show the hard work that had been put into its construction.

By the end of the month they had saved nearly fifty dollars. This was a mighty sum in this day. A sum equal to or exceeding the monthly mean. Complimented by the fact they had no overhead, little food cost, no clothing needs and free housing made them better off than most. Jimmie was already setting up plans to rent a room for them and to find their long lost kin.

When things are seem too good to be true; they usually are!

Chapter VII

Cop on the Block

Pittsburgh, as most large cities, had been sectioned into districts, wards and sides. The south side was home to one of the largest steel mills. Birmingham, Mt. Oliver and the heights were also in this ward. The north side was also sectioned into districts which in turn had wards and blocks. Blocks were the smallest unit identified by the city's agencies. Water distribution, power and streets were categorized by the 'block'. Accordingly, the police used the same technique in which to address crime as well as to allocate manpower. Yes, MANpower. There were NO women, no blacks and no Latinos on the entire police force in this time of sin.

Police were generally politically appointed by ward bosses, ranking officers or local politicians. Little or no training was required.

On the job education came quickly. Not all of the police were corrupt. Just most of them. Those not on the take were considered untrustworthy and never promoted. One in particular who refused to 'play ball' was given every rotten job that came along. He never complained instead performing to the letter of the law. He was a fine man who did his job with pride. All the other cops took payoffs, free meals and abused their powers. This one, of few, finally obtained major medical disabilities due to his dutiful performance. His reward was total denial of all benefits in spite of his 100% disability. This resulted in the very first ever lawsuit against the Pittsburgh Police. The award of $3000.00 was incidental compared to the changes the litigation caused. This was the catalyst for the Pittsburgh Police Officers Association, which would protect officers' rights without prejudice in the years to come.

The Three Italian Boys were not so lucky as to have this hero cop on their block. Instead they received one of the many huge Irish immigrants who obtained his job with the election of a town elder and countryman from their heavily populated district. The "cop on the block" ruled with an iron fist. In the real world this was rather a large wooden "night stick". The twirling of the night stick on its leather strap was a form of intimidation. This large stick alongside the huge size of the Irish cops was complimented by their known thirst for blood. Beating of petty thieves was the departments' method of keeping the criminals in line. Simply caught stealing a candy bar or apple could bless you with a broken arm or nose. Beatings were given on the spot with no appeals. Police brutality was never prosecuted during this time of American history.

If a serious crime, or that a respectable citizen was involved, then the shift sergeant was called in and the subject taken to the local police station. Every ward had a local precinct. Lord had no mercy on an Italian violator who was taken to a Irish dominated station for interrogation for any crime. Age had no privileges. A ten or twelve year old got beaten as bad as any adult. Often more so to impress the violator not to sin again. This 'cop on the block' was truly the judge, jury and executioner. To fight a cop would bring the wrath of hell upon the offender. A toot of his whistle brought every cop for blocks to the scene where there was no quarter given to a perpetrator . None of this had ever been explained to the "Three Italian Guys".

On their sales rounds of the fifth week, Victor was pushing while Jimmie doing his great sales on the lower north side when Officer O'Leary approached them. Sam was left behind to watch over their 'home' and goods.

"Top of the day to you lads." Said the extra large Irish cop.

"And to you Officer." Jimmie shot back.

"Do you care for a fresh orange or peach?"

"Don't mind if I do," as he took the pick of the wagon. "I've had a complaint or two that you've interfered with the local produce delivery man and Joes' Corner Market's sales."

"Oh, no sir. We only sell on the street."

"Yes but that takes business from the legitimate store owners; you're stealing their customers."

"What's legitimate mean?"

"Oh, people who pay taxes, business licensed and things like that." The cop slowly stated.

"Who do we have to pay?"

"Me." Replied Officer O'Leary with a smile.

"How much?" Jimmie countered.

"Let's say five dollars a week plus free groceries for my family. Delivered to my house, of course."

"That's more than we make!" Jimmie said.

"Bull crap, don't shit me boy! You pay nothing for this crap, sleep in that shack at the point free and pay nothing to nobody. You think life's free?"

"Who gives you the right to charge us?" Jimmie asked.

And with that Officer O'Leary struck Jimmie with his nightstick square on the side of the head causing blood to stream from his ear. Then the stunned Victor was next to catch the swing on his upper arm sending him flying knocking over the wheelbarrow into pieces.

"That's my right you stinking little wops! Next time I catch you, you'll both be in the hospital, got it?"

No one on the street had said a word. Messing with the cop on the block was a ticket to trouble. Soon the street was empty except for the two bleeders and their turned over cart which was destroyed. They quickly got up and retreated to their shack by the river. The cop had said he knew where they lived. Sammie was alone and he would take a major beating before giving up their homemade fort. They ran all the way back to the river leaving their goods for the vultures who were sure to descend from every door of every apartment. After explaining what had happened to Sam they packed their personal belonging in their orphanage blankets and filled the old duffle bag with their possessions. They were street wise enough to know the cops goon squad was sure to follow.

To supplement their meager incomes, some cops got part time jobs or worked overtime. Most other police took all types of payoffs. Not a lot but consistently. The corner store might pay a buck or two a month while a restaurant more if they required protection. Payoffs went up the ladder all the way to the captains, deputies and the chief himself. None were without sin. A tough captain in touch, such as Captain

McClusky, would retire on a wealthy corrupt pension.

This is how it was done prior to the governmental retirement and legitimate pension plans.

When the boys had traveled the inner streets of Pittsburgh to sell their leftovers, they had met with one of the few, fine Italian immigrants selling produce at the farmers market. He had been buying on consignment from a few local growers then selling at the market and from a small stand he had leased from his brother in law. This stand was not much better than the boys' former shack at the market. He was a fine hard working middle aged man who conversed with ease to the youngsters from his fatherland. Tony was only 29 years old.

"Why have you closed you shop Tony?"

"Had a problem with the local cop."

"Yeah so did we." Jimmie cited.

"So I heard, he burned you out, ah?"

"We got out just in time."

"Word around town is they also beat you."

"Yeah; guess word travels fast."

"Small town. Big gossip."

"So, what you going to do now?"

"I'm cooking at the family restaurant. We pay off a captain now. No one else bothers us."

"Yeah our cop wanted like five dollars a week."

"Same here, plus his entire family came for freebies. It was cheaper, and safer to close shop. Seems the bosses want to put all the small guys out of business and make the people buy at the newer supermarkets. Someone's getting paid big bucks."

"What are you going to do with your stand?" Jimmie asked.

"Just lock her up now. Not much to lose. All the value is in the land. Someday this lot will bring big bucks."

"Oh yeah. Great location only a block from the train station. How much you rent it for?"

"Tell you what. Clean up around here and straighten out the lot, you can stay free. Just no selling, ok?"

"You got a deal Tony."

"If you get hungry come by the restaurant. We close at 9 every night and I'll give you leftovers for cleanup work."

"See you at 9 boss."

So the cop on this block also squeezed all the little guys out of business. The establishment gave news releases and copy that the produce wagons and fruit stands were unhealthy and a public nuisance. They were all unlicensed, paid no taxes and exposed the community to health risk. Stories of the plague, Spanish Flu and other contagious diseases always accompanied the news giving credibility to the rationale of the rich and influential.

Authors note: (Never believe everything you read!)

Tony's fruit stand wasn't all that bad. Sure in the coming winter they would all freeze to death. For now the roof did not leak and the display bins made excellent above ground beds. They could lock the doors and it was close to everything. Most importantly the new train station was only a block away. The new grand rail station was huge. Railroads were the number one transportation of the day. To service the great number of passengers the transit authority, railroad companies and the federal government built "Stations for the future". Only the best material, from stone and marble to copper plumbing was permitted. Slate roofs, 16 to 20 foot high with stained glass ceilings and the best tile lavatories were appointed.

One by one and never as a group, the boys would enter and use the grand facility for their personal needs. The late night or wee hours of the a.m. were usually vacant. Even the lavatory was a kings palace compared to St. Paul's. Passenger trains were normally daytime arrivals and departures except for delayed schedules. Security habits, police presence and the stations operating system were all carefully watched by the three brothers. They took turns noting important issues. These boys were survivors with above average intelligence. Hard working souls are always watching for opportunities. It was plainly evident that the passenger's baggage was easily accessible to anyone who wished to take it.

A plan was quickly formulated.

If they did not take the luggage, someone else surely would.

Their surveillance would soon begin paying off.

Police were seldom at the station after 10 p.m., even though the delayed trains came in at all hours. A federal requirement stated the 'grand stations' would have to be open 24/7. During the day there was always a cop or two on duty. Railroad security also employed a few good men, but these were normally watchmen for stowaways or rail bums who didn't pay the fare or who hopped rides. These 'hobos', as they became known, stole rides from coast to coast free of charge. To control this misuse of the railroad, brutal rail workers with huge sticks, similar to the police night sticks, would routinely beat the hobos half (and sometimes totally) to death. Even police in the rail centers around the country took sport in whipping on the indigent.

Several terms grew from this disgusting behavior. The Billy was a English word for 'copper' (cop) and thus the "Billy club". A wider version on the club was also used and was called a bull's sized club. The word bully for the larger armed officer, who beat on the intimidated weak, became common.

The boys were products of a corrupt system. From the orphanage to the 'cops on the block' society failed its duty to protect, educate and care for those unable to care for themselves.

Soon they would have to survive any way they could.

Armed with the orphanage experience of thinking out their misdemeanors prior to execution, the boys soon were in a lucrative luggage theft business. Whenever a train came in late, the porters were never present. The boys, dressed and cleaned in their Sunday best, would assist the overburdened passengers for a few pennies or a nickel. They even used the dollies and wagons used during the day by the real porters. They worked hard and if they hustled a lot fifty cents to a dollar might be obtained in tips for their late night services.

Today's modern railroads and air travels still have the same "luggage lost" problems that have plagued transportation for centuries. Sometimes bags arrive late for their connection, or put on the wrong train. More often than not the bag may be tagged improperly for assignment. This would result in the bag being left on the passenger debarkation deck till the next morning when the day shift came to work. Late running trains were always in a hurry in unloading the luggage. Using the carts and push wagons, unclaimed baggage was simply wheeled out the front door and carried "home" to the fruit stand for "picking".

This was a treat in itself. Clothes and shoes were the major reward but jewelry, hats, cosmetics, cigarettes and booze were also found in the suitcases. Once a coin collection worth over $100 was found hidden between two 'Grand' hotel towels. All the loot they were taking required a "fence" (middle man). Tony had the perfect such friend in a small store on the south side. Not surprising was the travelers often packed away some excellent shoes of the highest quality. These sold for good money, as did the best of the clothing. Remember, it was the wealthy and those with money who could afford the train. Even the slightly used luggage demanded a good return.

Soon they were again making good money. Better than they could believe. $50, $60 even $70 a month and still they had free dinners after hours at Tony's for the kitchen cleanup, no rent and an ample supply of stock. Tony was receiving a kickback from the fence that now was brokering his oversupply to the other 'dealers'. Everyone took a few pennies and everyone seemed happy. Life was good.

Well perhaps not everyone was happy. It didn't take long for the railroads luggage department to figure out that a problem existed. Night security was beefed up and finally in the fourth month a cop was brought in for the dreaded graveyard shift. This had no stopping the "3 Italian Guys" as Tony and his family called them. Soon it was determined by the little three that the cop slept in a back room during his entire shift. Baggage taken from the platform was openly stored unsecured. The thefts became more difficult, but still without detection. They were now more careful with an eye out for the cop and railroad bullies.

Simply put, they were being set up. A little sting was conceived by the cop and a 'railroad dick'. Expensive leather luggage was left on the platform while the cop was usually sleeping at 2 a.m.. The boys came in to make their usual play, with Vic, being the slowest to move due to his large size, as the lookout. Jimmie and Sam saw no one in sight although the railroad bully tossed a rock on the roof of the cops sleeping quarters to alert him that the theft was in progress. The cop came running out, night stick in hand. (The standard large sized overfed Irishman as was common in the ranks.) He was furious at these young thieves operating on his turf and meant to punish them. Street justice was his and his alone, or so he believed. No one dared challenge his authority. His large Billy was ready to inflict the pain due these perpetrators.

"Justice shall be mine!" Screamed the red faced pissed off cop on the block.

He was not to do justice but rather to inflict pain on the punks whose thievery now required his late night shift. No bone would be left unbroken.

Right on cue, the giant cop came out of his room beside the platform and grabbed the unsuspecting Sammie by the back of his neck, striking him hard with his night stick across the legs trying to break them so he could not run away. Jimmie was a good six feet behind Sam and saw the pinch coming.

One of the stolen luggage items found by Jimmie earlier was a fine four inch switch blade. Jimmie never hesitated in pulling it out to stick the cop in the back. Sam was swinging, kicking and fighting for all he could. Sam was always a great fighter and the cop had difficulty holding him for a second hit with his club. It was then that Jimmie pushed the blade deep into the upper right shoulder blade of the uniformed cop. This caused the cop to drop his stick, releasing Sam and falling to his knees in pain. Blood gushed from the cop's upper shoulder blade as he screamed in agony.

In his haste to assist the cop the lookout had stumbled himself coming down the roofs fire escape. Having twisted his ankle, he was out of the hunt. Sam was not. He soon had the cops stick which had fallen and using it like a baseball bat beat the disabled cop severely. Legs, arms, ribs and nose were broken as the bleeding officer of the law who was now lying helplessly on the ground.

After retrieving the dropped bag they made for the exit. Surprisingly Vic was still on lookout.

"Help us with this bag."

"What happened?"

"We were ambushed by another cop."

They never waited for the sun to rise they packed everything they could carry and went to the "fence:", whose store was on the other side of the river. With over two hundred dollars, a great sum in this era, they began their quest to find their father and get out of town. There was no going back to the stand or market. Beating on the cop would be jail time for sure. Perhaps worse. Every cop in town would have their eye out for the 3 hooligans, or at least so they thought. In reality the cop was shamed by the ass kicking he had received by a couple of children. His report read there were three large thugs in their twenties who had jumped him. The railroad cop, also less then proud of himself, supported the cops tale. Both reputations would be ruined if the truth be told. Besides if they ever caught either of the thieves they surely would not live to talk of the incident. The word on the street was out. Railroad station thefts were now class one felonies in the eyes of the local cops, anyone caught with 'hot' goods was equally guilty and subject to "Police" brutality.

The game was over. At least for the "3 Italian Guys".

Chapter VIII

'Oh Little Town of Bethlehem'

Finding their father was not all that difficult. Jimmie simply went over to the unlimited Mine Workers union headquarters and told the young secretary he was looking for his father. He had dressed as the poor orphaned youngster he was and in the most of soft innocent tones stated:

"My mom has died and I must find Papa. Oh, please Miss help me." Jimmy said in tears.

It took a call or two, but she provided him with the location where Marshall was. He had received a crew leader's promotion and lived in a boarding house just outside the mine where he worked. His crew was all Italian immigrants and lived in the boarding house near the mines entrance.

New Bethlehem is less than 100 miles northeast of Pittsburgh; north of Kittanning, south of Clarion and west by 20 miles of the world famous Punxsutawney ground hogs home. The first oil was discovered in the United States less than fifty miles north. The area had some of the most gorgeous lands in the world. Thick changing forest, year round rivers and the richest soil anyone could want. Summers are humid, winters brutal but the falls and springs are what love is made of. New Bethlehem's Red Bank River that runs through the town lives up to its name. Thousands of years of mineral deposits have given the lush color to the valley itself. In the fall the billions of White Pine and Hemlocks turn majestic shades of yellows, reds and browns to compliment the rivers beauty. Coned pines and white capped mountains only add depth.

It is truly Gods' country.

The French were the first Europeans to visit the riches of Western Pennsylvania. Soon after the German influx was absorbed by the New Bethlehem area. Even today nearly half the population has German surnames or bloodlines. These strong hard working intelligent immigrant made the earth talk. New Bethlehem was founded over two hundred years ago by the name Gum town. The town has had a tough road to survival. Its river has flooded; time and again causing water contamination, (typhoid) in 1910, the loss of its glass foundry brewery, brickworks and saw mills. The coal mines disasters have left less than 1000 residents in a once bustling city.

Today the hardiest persist to live on the grounds of their forefathers. Fore fathers who dug the mines, built the factories and plowed the fields. This was the heart and soul of the industrialized America. Loyalty to family, God and country is inscribed on every citizen's guardian angel.

If you ever wish to show your children where America's greatness came from, don't take them to Jamestown, Boston or Washington, but rather Clarion County, Pennsylvania.

Servicing the area was the Buffalo, Rochester and Pittsburgh Railroad (BRPR). Rail was expanding quickly in the state for three compelling reasons. First and foremost, the mills required the coal and iron ore that were being mined to be transported to the steel city. Big dollars were being paid for delivery. Second were the tax benefits. Tax free and huge allowances were given the railroads by the state and federal government. Railroads were protected by laws that gave them near monopoly. Third was the incentive of lands and right of ways. Land was taken from thousands of citizens for little or no compensation giving the BRPR not only the right-of-way they required for the rails but large tracts of land to boot. All in the name of progress (spelled greed).

Even the spur tracks were given right of ways and free lands. These 'spurs' were side tracks to the mines making hauling the ore much easier. Huge coal bins were fitted for storage above the spurs tracks. The empty cargo car would be moved under the mines storage bins then loaded by gravity controlled levers. Once all the coal was loaded, accounted and signed for by the engineers, it was transported to satisfy the hunger of the smoking mills in Pittsburgh and beyond.

Many spurs were 'short' tracks or H.O. grade 40" tracks. These off size from the main rail were for mining use and owned by the companies.

From Pittsburgh, the BRPR headed north to another growth city, Butler Pass, before routing east through New Bethlehem and onto the then booming city of Punxsutawney. The groundhog day had yet to be invented but coal, ores, tile, gristmills, lumber and even its own brewery were in double shifts. Trains were running hourly and hopping a ride was relatively easy. So easy in fact that it became a type of a sport with the more adventurous. So many miners were hopping the coal trains the BRPR took few restricting measures besides; the workers were on their way to the mines to work. At least for the most part. The miners were the peasants and slaves of the industrialist. No reason to hinder their transport.

If nothing else, the '3 Italian Guys' were indeed 'adventurous'. The problem was that this train was not stopping in New Bethlehem, but going on through to Punxsutawney. As the train slowed in New Bethlehem the boys simply jumped off. Their young strong bodies took the fall well.

There are many types and sizes of coal mines. The disparity equals the range of clothes for sale at a department store. They begin with the smallest of family owned and operated diggings where wives and children were often required for the extraction. It grows from there.

On the other side of the coin is the huge mine employing thousands. These corporate holding were often the prize investments of railroads, steel companies and industrialists. Large properties were acquired as rails were laid and towns built by the owners. Often the towns were shacks and a general store, which were all owned by the mine. Entire cities have been (are) built over the coal shafts and underground digs. Decades later, with the development of large mechanical devices such as earth movers and steam shovels, strip mines came into being, reducing the need for the large scale human labor. These large mines often resulted in hundreds of deaths due to the unexplained explosions and cave-ins such in Marianna, Pa. or Cherry Hill. Flooding was another common cause of mine fatalities.

Less known are the thousands of coal mines that were (are) smaller than the corporate giants, but still larger than the 'ma and pa' types. These were both proprietor owned and contracted out. Some could employ hundreds while others only a dozen or so. Coal mines at the time, as today, often 'splintered' into several satellite mines producing from the same vein from different entry and exit locations.

Red Bank fit into the latter category.

The city of New Bethlehem was over twice the size it is today. Thousands were employed at the peak of the boom years in the counties coal industry alone. Miners dug, processed and exported billions of tons of coal to the mills south. Towns, cities and its people receive nothing from the mills carnage. The exploitation was unrestricted. The industrialist took what they wanted and left the spoils to contaminate for centuries to come.

Boarding houses were generally not in the cities or towns. Instead the mining companies built large rooming houses adjacent to the shaft opening on company property. Timber taken from the land was milled on site and used for the construction. Local river rocks and stone were the foundations. Most did have indoor plumbing. One bath upstairs for the 16 or so miners and one on the first floor for the housekeeper, supervisor and family. Unlike today's norm, many miners would ride the rail, stay for 5 to 10 days to work and return to the city. Mostly crew leaders and shift bosses lived in the B & Bs.

The pick miner was the backbone of coal mining for the first 2000 years. Yes, 2000. Smelter and mines dating back to 200 B.C. have been found in Chinas deepest interior. Then and into the late 19th century the "man powered pick" was the primary method of taking the coal, ore or gems from the earth.

This method was certainly the choice at the Red Bank Mines. However, miners were not only paid by production and not hourly, but that were also required to purchase their own tools and lamp fuel. Kerosene and picks were of course sold at predatory prices by the company store, where "script" of course was accepted. Ropes, work boots and heavy duty 'dungarees' were also priority items sold at the company stores.

Graft, theft and scams were commonplace. Stealing or 'misappropriating an immigrants hard earned coal vouchers by management happened more often than not. Motley McGuiness, Irish based thugs, hired out to "protect the miners" became the first unionization for the miners. Yet the criminal element had no skills or management beyond intimidations or beatings. That would change decades later.

All the while the immigrant coal miners worked their bodies to the bone.

Miner's boarding houses were in fact quickly built company owned non compliant shacks. There were no building codes or inspectors. Most were built in a week's time. No sheet rock or insulation was used. Single wall construction with the local pine as the walls and ceiling was common. Even the roof was Pine over 2 x 4's, with a metal top. This roof was very loud in heavy rains. Heat was from three major sources. A large fireplace, wood burning stove and body heat were utilized. Body heat of 16 miners and perhaps another four residents gave off a lot of heat in a 800 square foot, two story building.

Still, the idea of a roof over your head, running water and good hot meals gave credibility to the boarding house. No commute time, utilities or standard rental problems made the boarders happy campers.

Water was usually run by a pipe from a nearby spring or creek. Natural springs are very common in the area and in fact became a problem with flooding when mine shafts crossed nature's way. Readily available drilling equipment, dug wells when required. Many 'dry hole' or unused coal mines were often used for sewage dumping.

Bunk 'beds and breakfast' were a treat for many who were known to have worked for far less without these benefits. Today's bed and breakfast are a far cry from the miner's boarding house.

These were forerunners to today's luxury B & B's. Not for pleasure mind you but rather need. Two large meals a day were served one at 8 a.m. and at 4 p.m. Bag lunches were also available for those on 12 hour shifts. These had sandwiches, fruit and a drink in them. Meals depended on the skill and good will of the innkeeper. The meals were gourmet compared to the limited rations obtained at the orphanage.

There were over one thousand mines in the western Pennsylvania area. Each mine had its own distinct name. Mail, locations and identification were determined by "given" names and by address. Present day mine maps dating back 150 years confirm and retain these very same designations. Local postmasters and freight dispatchers knew the locations even though they were spread over a wide area. Very few outside the state mine agency knew where each mine was in fact located. The mines themselves were not mapped by the Pennsylvania Bureau of Mines (BMR) until 1930, and updated in 1998. Prior to 1930 each mining company had the responsibility of charting and recording their own diggings. The charting was declared a very low priority by the companies, leaving mines uncharted for nearly 100 years. So much for allowing the honor system to function properly.

This same indifference carried over to the mine owners contaminated dumping, cross shafting, river and stream pollutions and uncontrolled burning; to name only a few of their sins.

Historically it is known that even the French and Germans had mined in this area. Present day Saltsburg produced for a century. Other cities named for their products in the area are Oil City, Clays town, Beaver Falls and Glassport. The cities remain today, surviving in spite of their raw materials being exhausted or no longer feasible for production. Played out, long abandoned mines litter the tri-state area resulting in constant dangers.

Records do exist for coal mines in the western Pennsylvania region dating back prior to the Civil War. Most of these maps are primers and without substance. Accurate angles of drilling, departments and map locations were developed without modern day methods. Few draftsmen had ever gone down deep into the mines taking accurate measurements. Miners naturally followed the veins. Their diggings could take them in any direction while the programmers had no idea where they had in reality gone. This is what caused and continues to cause, cave-ins, flooding and cross mining. Many cities, including Pittsburgh and New Bethlehem along with hundreds of others, were built on top of mines. Many of the mines would collapse, catch fire or flood causing the devastation to the buildings built above them. Sink holes, foundation failures and condemned structures are common in the Ohio, Pennsylvania and West Virginia region.

Three major types of mining prevail to this day. Shaft mining is the best known, where 'shafts' or holes are dug into the ground in order to extract the product. In many locations the minerals are in hills or mountains where 'drafters' can plan, map and engineer the extractions for a perpendicular angle. This was the preferred, when available method. After WWII and the development of huge earth movers of the strip mining was introduced and widely used especially in the subject region. This excavation totally stripped the earth of its outer shell down to the sought after minerals. Many states and nations have outlawed strip mining. Millions of acres of America have been permanently destroyed by this type of stripping, even though it is the most cost effective of the methods. It is also the safest for the miners although it employed far fewer workers.

A third popular method is a type of surface grading. When the coal or ore is close to the surface the earth can be graded, allowing open exposure to the sought after material. Unlike the deeper strip mine "open faced" mines are more easily restorable to their natural condition. It is much safer than shaft mining permitting all the employees to work above ground.

New Bethlehem, as nearly all the local mines, was of the shaft type. Modern day mechanical and safety measures were generally unheard of. Power driven lifts, electric cars and motorized drills or digging equipment were non-existent. This resulted in man power doing nearly all the excavations and shaft diggings. Only the strong and conditioned need apply. Weaker men's time on the job was short lived. It was (is) a dirty, nasty job. It was also quite dangerous.

The danger however was not limited to the coal miners. Cities, towns, homes, churches and schools were built above and beside the mines and its shafts. This undermining created unsafe living conditions. Sink holes, tilting structures and underground fires, persist to this day. Residents of smaller rural towns such as New Bethlehem in Clarion County Pennsylvania have lived with the sins of the mines for 100 years. Pittsburgh's own suburbs such as Castle Shannon, Brookline, Lebanon and Mt.

Washington fear no less. In Brookline alone, a middle class town of smart brick two story homes, chances are better than ten to one that the residents live over an abandoned mine.

Other crimes were (are) also committed upon those unsuspecting residents. Coal dust, mill smoke and polluted water supplies were by-products of the industrialist. Families of the miners were subject to the same cancers, black lung and other man made terminal illnesses as the miners themselves. It would take decades to even begin cleaning the air and rivers. Much longer to heal Mother Earth.

For a few pennies more the Pittsburgh region could have been spared eternal pollution. True, the rich got richer.

All in the name of greed not need.

In addition to the multiple types of cancers and contaminates being produced there were also the dreaded miners "damp" syndromes. These killers were (are) given names to relate their deadly characteristics to each deadly disease.

"White" damp was related to the unseen white' carbon dioxin which strangulates and deprives the miners of oxygen. "Black" damp was the deadly dust and lung contaminate. Damp "stink" was formulated from the sulfur and caused not only respiratory ailments, but continual nausea from the "rotten egg" odor. Damp "fire" was related to the methane gas

"The Original Mines"

which was constant in most every mine. "After" damp is a recurring carbon-nitrogen combination that either blew up the entire mine or the miners' throat and lungs for the rest of their lives.

Another side effect of the multitude of illnesses was alcoholism. To flush the coal dust down and ease the pain of toxins alcohol was the readiest of suppressants. Habitual drinking became commonplace. Miners hid their bottles in every imaginable place. Thousands of great minds, souls and hearts were lost to the "lies" that the miners were safe. Steel mills, processing plants and local industries were no safer. Dust, silt, smog and slag destroyed the greatest America had to offer. Family trees and DNA continues to suffer to this day.

Hideous working conditions, long hours and mining company rules gave the workers no security. Production quotas had to be met. The pay per hour was low with no benefits. Miners unions were low on the totem pole of civil rights priorities. Governmental oversight was non-existent. The corporation and industrialist did most anything they wished. The mines were dirty beyond ones wildest imagination. The coal dust took its toll from head to foot. Skin received melanoma and squalors cell cancers. Respiratory systems also came under attack from all the damp, dust and particles containing dioxins. Black lung, throat cancer and related disorders took more than a fair share of miners. Eyes and nose membranes were also constantly choked by the dust. Small round eye goggles gave raccoon looking images to the miners as they exited the shafts. (Literally). Permanent damage to nasal passages was also commonplace with the union members who had no medical coverage.

Danger is a fact of life with a miner and his family. In every country and corner of the world the fear of tragedy is a constant. A lack of concern for the miner coupled with the greed for profit gives great peril to the underground servants of the mines. Cheap timbers, poor planning, drainage problems and irresponsible management led to death and worse. The worst, the ones who have never been recovered.

Lost forever in the pitch black hole of shaft mining; now that's a true sin.

Oxygen deprivation and gas explosions were also major concerns causing numerous deaths. Suffocation is a terrible threat to live with every day.

Every miner knew well of his harm's way. This created a bonding by miners groups. The smaller the group the stronger the bond. A crew consisted of perhaps a half dozen or so while the group included several crews. The shift was that mines total manpower for a given time. Ten or twelve hour shifts were common. Most individual mines had a strange sense of ethnocentrism. If a fight broke out in a local bar you could always count on your mine buddies backing you up. Crews worked, ate, slept. And died together.

Employers used this loyalty to their own advantage by shaming one mine by another's higher production. In truth this was ridiculous. Some coal and ore are closer to the surface. Content and types all had variable factors for extraction.

Once off the coal train the brothers found New Bethlehem to be a two story brick city of hardly a dozen square blocks with a river running through it. After surviving the streets of Pittsburgh this would be a piece of cake, or so they thought.

Their first problem was locating the boarding house. All they had was the name of the mine and New Bethlehem. It could be a wild goose chase, but that wasn't likely. Anyhow all they could lose was time, and that they had plenty of.

Jimmie used his youthful wit and went directly to the largest bar in town. (There were a dozen bars for each church, thus the need for New Bethlehem's own brewery.) His brothers waited outside as he entered.

"Excuse me sir." he said to the bartender, "Could you tell me where the Red River Mine number one is?"

"No son, but I'm sure those gents over there will." as the tender pointed to the corner table. "Hey Brent, where's the Red River Mine at?" It's west of town, down the rail on Hensley Road by Cottage Hill." Brent yelled back.

"Thank you sir." Jimmie replied and left.

There were no street signs or markers. New Bethlehem and Clarion County had no need for them. People in this region have always reached out to help others. They all knew where their neighbors lived.

The dirt road was rough and full of potholes. Winter snows and heavy seasonal rains help to roughen it. Deer, bear or perhaps a beaver could jump out of the darkness at any time. Victor, the youngest, had never seen such blackness and didn't like it one bit.

It was nearly 9 p.m. when the bright lights of the Red River Mine came into sight. Just as they were told, the large faceless straight gray two story boarding house sat next to the shafts main entrance. Although the lights on the shaft were stadium bright, the house appeared dark, perhaps vacant.

The knock on the door was repeated several times before their father answered the door.

"Hi dad." Victor yelled to a wine laced, half clad man.

"What the hell!"

"We came up to see you!" Victor yelled.

"Poor miner's town"

"Why aren't you in school?"

"They weren't schooling us dad. That was a slave driven prison."

With that Rose, now eight months along turned on the lights and welcomed her brothers. They were in awe over her obvious condition. This resulted in an all night discussion; it was agreed upon that Rose had to be given support for her delivery and upbringing of the soon to be born. Presently the mines and owner all loved her, the food and manner in which she kept the boarding house. Even the owner/manager marveled at her work ethic and ability to run the boarding house. Food was delivered on a company contract from a local vendor. Fresh meats, poultry, vegetables, milk and fruit came daily. Utilities were next to nothing and the company built house had no other cost. Residents pay was debited accordingly for their boarding. Rose was paid $5 a month plus the free room and board for herself, father and soon to be born. The rough male tenants gave her total respect besides her father was not only large but also their crew chief. When you work nearly a mile underground and your life depends on your crew, the most of respect is given everyone, especially the chief.

Every crew member decided to accompany Marshall and the boys to the Pittsburgh mansion to demand justice for Rose. Her honor, the child's well being and their Italian pride were all at stake. Sunday morning they jumped the loaded Pittsburgh bound BRPR train for the ride to the big city. They were armed with justice on their side, lots of anger and several bottles of cheap homemade hooch. (Every mine had its own hooch maker.) By the time they reached the mansion on Pittsburgh's north side, they were all painless. A large iron gate separated them from the main house. A Pinkerton security guard confronted the 'gang' and told them to move on or he'd have them beaten. Since the

"Homestead" massacre the unions hatred for the Pinkertons was as bad as it gets.

As the Pinkerton guard argued at the front gate with the hooligans, Jimmie and two of the youngest miners flanked the guard. To the far right and out of his sight, they scaled the black six foot wrought iron fence. Coming up behind the guard they overpowered him and opened the gate for the dozen coal miners to enter. In an instant they were pounding on the solid 12 foot high front double doors of the huge stone home. When no one dared to answer they began tossing their wine and beer bottles through the windows. Family and staff alike were in fear for their lives. All exited the main houses rear door to the safety of the Pinkertons guard house where the outnumbered four on duty stood with their sticks and a shotgun ready to repulse an attack. The fear of God had blessed their souls for life.

Finally the first of the alerted police arrived to calm the disturbance. The police were still outnumbered by the hooligans. The only Italian Sergeant on the scene asked what the problem was. Hearing Marshall out, the sergeant gained their confidence and had moved them all off of the property.

The alcoholic mob was pushed back onto the street just as the cavalry arrived with a dozen more of Pittsburgh's finest. The sergeant explained the situation to both his colleagues and the Pinkerton supervisor who had also called for help. Dozens of Pinkerton 'Reserves' were on their way.

Police dislike child molesters more than most. They see the results and devastation caused by a sickos need for self satisfaction. A pregnant 12 year old would be reason enough for any of them to seek justice. Even the Pinkerton in charge agreed, not knowing it was the master himself responsible for the sin. All they were certain of was that she had worked there, only had sex with one man and now was with child.

It was Butler who finally emerged. Everyone thought he must be the culprit. With the sergeant and Pinky closely watching it was agreed that a $50 fee be paid now for the childs birth and $8 a month till the child was 18 years of age. This innocent employee took the blame for his perverted employer.

For 18 years the payments were made from the master's private account. His wife and staff all knew the truth. She would later divorce him, having been disgraced the entire time they were married. Finally, she could take no more. Their son, the brightest bead on the Rosary, was raised in San Francisco, California. The master was never prosecuted.

The miners returned by empty coal train that very night celebrating their victory. The Pinkerton had been confronted and they were all in one piece. Justice, at least a little portion of it, had been served. On their walk back up the old dirt road they picked flowers for Rose.

This Pittsburgh sin could have ended here. It was however natural for any child with the DNA of such a successful person to strive him or herself. Many born out of wedlock pursue their biological parents. Tracing ones roots can become a passion with many. Today's DNA can be the basis of proof of survivorship and even legal beneficiaries to the wealth left by their parents.

This road would lead to hell.

"Boarding house on coal tracks"

Chapter IX

A Child is Born

The next day Jimmie confessed to his father about stabbing the cop who was beating on his brother.

"This was not really a bad thing. Cops are all corrupt." Was his father's reply.

"Yes but I don't feel safe around here. Especially now that the Pittsburgh cops know where we are at."

"What's your plan?" Rose asked.

"I like riding the rail. I'm going to see the country."

"And money?"

"We saved some good money. Besides I can always work on the road for a meal or two." With that he split up the money evenly with his two brothers, packed his own hobos gear and jumped the next train headed west. He always wanted to see Chicago, New Orleans and eventually even Florida.

And so he would, riding every train in every direction except for Pittsburgh. Always in fear for his crime and the prosecution for the stabbing he never did return, even though no one was really looking for him. Eventually he'd settle in a beautiful seaside town he found in Virginia where he happily married and raised his own fine family.

Three weeks later Rose had a healthy son. The delivery cost her $30 paid to a midwife who lived in New Bethlehem. The following day Rose made both the house meals for the crew and cleaned the house. She was a natural mother, breast feeding, wiping and rocking like a saint.

Rose also kept her religious beliefs as well as retaining her perfect figure and self well groomed.

"Rose inside the boarding house"

Self confidence gave her the ability to cope with the worst of life and come up smiling.

With Jimmie gone on his rail hopping, Vic and Sam slept in the supply pantry while Rose, the baby and Marshall used the bedroom. The well kept child seldom, if ever, cried. Rose was never out of his sight. This sense of total security allowed the child to rest with love always on his shoulder. There was never a need to be loved, changed or fed, therefore there was never a need to cry.

Instead of a nuisance the crew accepted the child as their 'adopted'. Never a cruel word was said to Rose or her child, who the crew nicknamed "Little Red River". He was taken on as a mascot. Loved by all with the care of an entire family. The child was now loved as if their own.

Several months after the child was born word was delivered that the owner/manager would be arriving from Pittsburgh in a few days.

Rose prepared a special midday meal of fresh beef, potatoes, carrots, celery with all the right spices and trimmings. Her stew was spectacular. She knew this to be his favorite meal and so it was set.

At first the 'boss' was concerned with the amount he was paying to Rose's two younger brothers. He wanted to cut their pay in half. Rose, who kept the books showed him the 10% increase in production for a one percent payroll increase. Besides the boys had no fear and with their small size were able to crawl into weakened shafts to secure headers or verify if the vein ran in that direction or not. They were great assets she argued and he agreed after verifying the production record. Both boys were still pre teens (Labor laws be damned.)

As crew chief, Marshall was invited to the family dinner with Rose, Sam and Victor. The boss sat next to Rose with Marshall and his boys flanking him on the opposite side of the table.

Two bottles of fine red wine was served and they all ate and drank into the evening hours. The boss, two sheets into the wind, kept showering Rose with compliments for her bookkeeping, boarding home management and motherhood. He managed six other mines and this was the best by far. His eyes never left her bosom which had grown with the blessing of motherhood.

Marshall was also snockered having opened up a third bottle of spirits. It was then that Rose felt the bosses hand on her upper thigh under the table concealed to all. She politely removed his hand the first time but when it happened again she said ever so softly,

"Don't ever try that again."

Now this was 'the boss', she was an employee, unmarried, with child and at his beck and call; or so he thought.

The third time was a charm. This time the half drunk ran his hand all the way up underneath her skirt. She was ready for him and with her fork in a quick strong stabbing motion pushed the prongs into his upper thigh. Pain and shock sobered him up quickly. If her father or brothers had known of these advances they'd surely have stomped his ass and they would all be fired. Good workers were tough to find. Bosses easier. All he could do was sit there in pain holding his wounded leg praying it wouldn't bleed too badly. He quickly covered the wound with his napkin and excused himself before leaving.

The incident would never be mentioned again. Rose and her father, with his crew, remained working the mine for over six years. The boss never returned.

At that time the new miners union came to town requiring everyone to join up and pay dues. Some went on strikes others vandalized mine equipment. Steel mills began forced slowdowns requiring less coal. The domino effect started a regional recession. Sam and Vic, both at the ripe age of 12, began paying union dues to the United Mine Workers.

Victor went on to become a head machinist in a steel fabrication plant near Pittsburgh. He also married and had children. Sam became a steel miller and iron worker. He married well and fathered five children. Victor and Sam both paid union dues for over fifty years.

Victor was elected shop foreman and the union representative for his factory. Every paycheck he matched the company maximum for a stock retirement fund. Shortly before he retired the company filed for federal bankruptcy when it was discovered management was in fact embezzling all the employees' contributions for all those years. Every dollar Victor had worked to save for his retirement had been stolen.

Sam became an iron workers foreman and ran several large jobs for the best of companies.

Like his father and brothers, he inherited the taste for alcohol. His choice of poisons took its toll.

After killing himself for over thirty years in the coal mines, Marshall contracted the dreaded black lung disease and died after years of painful convalescent. Never a cent of disability, workman's compensation or unemployment was ever collected. Even his medical cost were denied in a time that big businesses got away Scott free by denial. American justices, fairness and equal rights were rigged scales 100 years ago. The Lady of Justice eyes and scales were indeed blind. Many a miner died penniless and destitute after a lifetime of the hardest labor on earth.

Meanwhile Rose had a real purpose in life. She had a child. Not just any child. One with fantastic good looks, tall, strong and the genes from a very intelligent father. Her constant care was priceless. The child grew with the confidence of a king. All the time Rose worked at the boarding house she also did 'extras' for the residents. This included washing their clothes, mending holes and preparing special lunches for the cave workers. Each chore would bless her with a nickel here or a dime there. The miners were far from wealthy but they appreciated with great respect the young mother and her services. Besides, she was a beautiful flower which lit up their entire day as they would exit the depths of hell. She could perhaps be their own sister, daughter or even wife if they could be ever so lucky.

Extra money from 16 or so miners added up to more than her child support monthly allotment of $8. Her job gave her room and board leaving her with no expenses. The boss, now ashamed of his drunken behavior had given Rose a raise and sent her nice clothes and gifts on a regular basis. As a seamstress Rose made the already expensive materials into a classy wardrobe. She never hesitated in the tailoring of the clothes into baby items for her son. These clothes likewise were better then the best of store bought available.

At the end of nearly seven years of 24/7 work Rose had saved every dime she had earned. She deposited the $7.50 per month boarding house salary into the same account as the $8 child allotment. This and the gratuities for her extra work allowed her to save over $25 per month. When the mine closed during the depression, Rose had over $2000. A very hefty sum for a 19 year old in the early 1900's.

When the mills in Pittsburgh closed over the coming years, nearly everyone was out of work. In the Pittsburgh region alone unemployment was over 40 percent. Houses were vacant and cheap. The stock market had crashed and big financiers were jumping out of windows. Money was king and Rose was the queen of the ball.

Large homes built for $5000 were on the market for less than $3000. Even these houses were not selling. Boarded up homes brought vandalism, squatters and bank losses. Rose was only familiar with the Pittsburgh's North Side of town which was (is) a short walk across the river into downtown Pittsburgh. One area in particular caught her fancy. Today it's called the Spanish War streets where several blocks remain on the city's historical listing. The one she selected was a huge two story dark reddened brick, 4000 square foot home with exquisite hardwood floors, banisters and wall trim. The ceilings were 12 to 16 feet tall with the entire kitchen capped with a copper shield. The roof was 'lifetime' slate. It was (is) a great building and a short walking distance to her former employer's mansion, a Roman Catholic cathedral, parks and schools.

The house was owned by a bank, as many were at the time. One can only imagine the bankers surprise when the poor immigrant walked in and offered $2000 cash for a $5000 house, which had already been discounted to $3000. Rose dressed her best and showed up flanked by her brother Sam and coughing father. Even the Sunday best they wore could not meet the bankers worst. She gave the address and her own account number to verify the funds were available. The banker smiled broadly.

"I'm very sorry ma'am but we don't work like that. The house is already discounted and that's our price."

Now Rose hadn't one tenth the banker's education. Nor he one tenth of the hair on her ass.

"Do you have a manager?"

"Of course." he replied.

"Let's see if he wishes to keep his job."

The manager was also a vice president of the bank and seemed annoyed to be called upon for his golden abilities. (Or so he believed).

"Yes ma'am, may I be of assistance."

Now Rose had ambushed both in the bankers. She knew they had hundreds of empty foreclosures, no buyers and cash flow problems of their own. Here sat this nineteen year old, stunning in looks, dressed for a ballroom dance and escorted by two obvious coal miners, trying to match wits with the city's richest.

"The house on Rebecca Place has been vacant for nearly two years. Windows are broke, wiring missing and in decay. I have cash and have offered it to you. You'll spend a fortune to repair whatever might be left of it."

"We thank you, but that's not quite enough. Say if you'd give us $2500 we might consider it."

"No, $2000 is my cash offer; else I'm going across the square and buy the house on the same street from the Mellon Bank. Then I'll write your board of directors and tell them why your house is still vacant and the other bank has my cash."

"Well here's the file on the property. Let me see. We loaned $2500 on it. They made ten payments of $50 each. We have interest, carrying cost and bank fees for a fair amount of $3000.

"Yes, but if you hold it another year, fix the electrical and still don't sell it, you're worse off. Besides the interest, bank fees and carrying are cost of doing business as you write it all off. $2000, take it or leave it."

The bankers took the deal and Rose, Sam, Victor, Marshall and the child moved in the very next day. Only a couple items had been left but the boys cleaned it up, fixed the broken windows and secured it in record time. It was and remains a grand ole' house that would cost $1,000,000 to replace. (Just not on Pittsburgh's North Side.)

Chapter XII

Steel City, USA

Rose had very little of her hard earned savings left after the purchase of their home. Victor, Sam and her father gave her all they had, but even this couldn't feed the family. With the mills closed work was nearly non-existent. Government "work project" was implemented to ward off riots and starvations. Marshall, now called "Nuni" in his new role, eventually obtained a job laying the bricks to the streets of Pittsburgh. This back breaking job was made more difficult with "Nuni's" black lung disease.

Meanwhile Victor and Sam worked day and night on Rose's house. They repaired windows, painted inside and out, sanded and varnished floors and scavenged furniture from every possible source. Junk piles and public dumps were their main success. Chest of drawers, chairs, broken tables and even box springs and mattresses were carried home. Piece by piece, old blinds, soiled drapes, pots, burned pans, lumber scraps and old rugs were lugged home. When the pickings got slim the boys began entering vacant boarded up, foreclosed homes by prying off the outside plywood security panels. Once inside they took anything and everything. Toilets, sinks, furniture, rugs, windows, oak railings, old clothes and torn sheets were all subject to confiscation if it had been left behind.

"Nuni's" bricklaying and the boys pilfering continued for nearly three years. Rose's garage and entire cellar was packed from floor to ceiling with "found items" (or so they referred to all the loot). Other houses nearby had begun to sell and the boys were soon employed by the new owners in making their renovations. The boys had also 'found' paint, brushes and supplies at the vacant homes. These they put to good use and received a fair price for from their employers. One new owner had agreed to pay the boys ten dollars to paint the interior and ten dollars to paint the exterior. When the job was completed the man gave them only half the agreed price. This was indeed a big mistake. That night the unoccupied house had graffiti, broken windows and total vandalism blessed upon the greedy owner. A licensed contractor was brought in who repaired the house a second time. That very night the house was once again totally vandalized. The same contractor came a second time for the third renovation. Halfway through the job all the new paint and materials were stolen from the secured job site. Then a 'live in' security man was employed to stay on the job. The night after the fourth renovation was completed the boys 'tattooed' the entire front of the house with obscenities. Then they tossed bricks through the windows scaring the hell out of the sleeping guard.

Every one of the neighbors knew exactly who and why the vandalism occurred. It was street justice. They also knew that they had to live next to the boys and to cross them was surely not in their best interest. The man had done them wrong and he was paying for it. Not by the courts, but rather vigilante style. Finally the man gave up and sold the house at a large loss. The new owner, after talking to the neighbors, hired the boys to repair the same damage for fifty dollars each. He willingly paid the completed job and lived there for years with never a problem.

All this time, Rose was devoting her time to her son and keeping an immaculate home. Her home had (has, it still stands) a tile vestibule entry. Here she made all to enter to remove their shoes. Two sets of slippers were available for special guests but family simply walked the house in 'socked feet'. Her varnished hardwood floors and tiled kitchen shined like the harvest moon. Even though the heat for the house was generated by four wood burning fireplaces, dust was non-existent. As a family project Rose, her father and two brothers repaired, refinished and built all the furnishings for the house. Rose reupholstered a grand old couch while the boys rewired steel coiled spring beds.

The kitchen had come with the latest 'wood fired' stove and ice box. A 2 cent hunk of ice would keep the cooler cold for a week. The stoves fuel was a bit more difficult to keep supplied. Logs had to be cut and of hard wood for the best of results. Procurement, hauling and splitting required a constant attention. Wood stoves and their exhaust stacks are notorious for distributing large amounts of heat. Whereas this was enjoyed during the coolest three seasons, it was a true burden in the summertime when cooking.

Although the plumbing was relatively new, Pittsburgh's water and sewage system carried most of the heavy duty. The real problem was the electrical. Electricians were then, as now, a sought after trade. Good, energetic, skilled, honest electricians were (are) in great demand. Unions now dominated all of Pittsburgh's trades. Carpenters, plumbers, electricians, painters, hotel workers, pipe fitters, heavy equipment operators, railroad workers and even the police now had unions. Top hourly wages were demanded and received. Years too late for many a coal miner.

Nuni and her brother hadn't the needed skill to repair the electrical and make it right in the large house. Pittsburgh was growing. Large multi story brick buildings were being built in the central downtown area. Zero lot line back to back row brick homes were also going up in the north, south and the hill sides of towns. Nuni had lots of work, as did the boys. Yet none of them had the electrical skills required for the house repairs.

In every neighborhood there exists a network of skilled workers known and trusted by the residents. Good food, produce, clothing and one's every need is neighborhood news exchanged daily. Roses' call for an electrician was echoed with three private names. The first to appear was a union worker who did side jobs for extra money.

"You need all new updated wiring. I can do it for $500 plus materials of say $200 or $300." He had stated.

Rose had asked him twice to remove his shoes which he shrugged off and laughed at the very idea.

The second referral never did show up.

A third was an independent gentleman of class. He never hesitated removing his shoes even before being asked. He was clean cut and although not of Italian decent he spoke some Italian obtained from his trade and former military service. Nuni loved the military stories. Harry, the electrician, had served in the US cavalry and had incredible stories. He also had a keen eye for the young and beautiful Rose.

Rose had not dated or ever gone out. She was a devoted mother with the highest of inborn instincts. Her calling was of family and not to party. Likewise Harry had never 'chased the skirts'. Up to now electrical wires and horses had been his bride. Until this moment he had hardly kissed or dreamed of a woman. Chemistry in love making is the most powerful of elements.

"Nuni" chaperoned Rose and Harry on their first date to a fine local Italian red and white checkered table clothed restaurant. Vic and Sam stayed at home to baby sit. "Nuni" drank all the wine, tossed down the food and quickly excused himself for the two block walk back home. So much for the chaperone. Still Harry was the gentleman. He knew Rose had a child but not the circumstances behind it. They talked till the waiter locked the doors. It was agreed at dinner that in exchange for Harry's electrical work, Rose would give Harry the rear garage rent free. Harry had no doubt that Rose made all the decisions in this family.

Some couples simply make a beautiful marriage. Rose's stunning looks and natural poise were mateched with Harry's being not only a handsome, healthy young man, but also well respected in the community. He could converse in Italian, German, Spanish and French. His cleanliness was surpassed only by his politeness that was genuine. Everyone enjoyed his quiet, but quick wit. Their courtship was nonsexual but still intense. "Nuni" readily accepted Harry. Besides many of Harry's customers blessed him with steaks and roast which Rose prepared for the entire family.

Large weddings were not a priority to Rose. They were married six months later in a simple chapel ceremony. Harry moved in that night and never left "till death did they part". Shortly prior to the marriage both Victor and Sam had moved out of the Rebecca Place home. Victor had secured a steel workers position in a new plant south of town. Pittsburgh's mills were burning once again and there were more jobs than employees. Big money had bet on the revitalization of the steel city with the smart money playing big.

Victor was to stay at that same fabrication mill for over fifty years. As a hard worker, he was rewarded by being elected shop steward and later union vice president. Still he worked and saved. The union had negotiated a retirement plan for each worker to which the worker also contributed a portion of his salary. Victor married, had children and was doing well until it was disclosed that the mills management had embezzled all the unions' retirement fund and was now bankrupt. Victor was devastated. A life time of work lost to the rich and now infamous.

Sam fared a little better. He first worked as a US steel worker. From the mill he obtained an apprenticeship in the iron workers union.

"Rose's only husband in uniform"

The iron workers are generally involved in heavy construction. This includes steel beaming high rises, bridge construction, and highway development, iron reinforcement and anywhere else steel or iron was used in the building trades. Union control of the trade was totalitarian. As his younger brother did, Sam married, had five children and did eventually receive a union pension.

With her brothers gone, "Nuni" took the master bedroom at the head of the stairs. The room had a fireplace for heat and the bathroom was right next to it. Rose's son was now ten years old and was also given a nice private room. Harry and Rose took the master bedroom on the first floor with its own private bathroom. "Nuni's" black lung worsened. He would sit or lie in bed for years before he was defeated by the miner's dreaded diseases.

Harry always treated Rose's son as if he were his own. The affection was one sided.

Knowing Harry was not his real father was only a part of the equation. His mother had been solely his possession for ten years and now he had to share her. This outsider also shared a bed with his saintly mother. The sounds and grunts coming from their room were disgusting. With this hatred came resentfulness. Harry could do nothing to reach out to the smart son of another. Rose and Harry both tried individually and as a couple to bring the rebel under control.

It never was successful.

Rose had put all the accounting skills she had acquired into Harry's business. He was a great electrician but a terrible accountant. Rose found hundreds in uncollected monies, set up bid sheets, consolidated contracts and soon had Harry making more money than he ever dreamed of. Besides, Harry was now doing what he enjoyed and did best; electrical work. He had always despised paperwork and thanked the lord for the accountant he had married. His little company would expand, hire sub-contractors and became a highly regarded Pittsburgh business. With her son now in the best private schools, Rose devoted her time to the business and her home. Harry in the mean time, frustrated with his stepson, became more and more of a workaholic. He took all jobs, large or small. Rose had enough to buy several homes but instead dressed her son in the very best and sent him to the finest schools available.

Rose and Harry remained close. Real close. They had total respect for one another. Neither had been one to go out or party. They worked, ate at home and enjoyed each other's company. Harry's business never caused friction. This was due to the separation of responsibilities as well as Harry being out in the field while she held down the office. He knew she could (and did) handle any problem that came along. She knew his work and integrity were so far above the norm that the few problems that did come along were insignificant.

"A love made in Pittsburgh."

Chapter XIII

Pittsburgh's Injustice

Harry was a parent but never a father. This was never Harry's fault. He had attempted involvement in every aspect of the child's rearing. The child knew Harry was not his natural father. As he grew older his inquiries became more and more brazen. During his high school years he had kept himself busy with girls, sports and grades. Besides an occasional fist fight or two he seldom was in any trouble. Still his temper was short and his tall body strong, never broad or large boned he still was a head above most of his classmates. That was until he was accepted, after graduation, and entered the University of Pittsburgh.

At the higher level of education he had more challenges, more time for thought, more need for answers. In one of his first semester social classes the subject of family genes and heredity was addressed. This was the match that lit the candle. Years of thoughts of not knowing came to the forefront.

Who was his real father? Why had he left his beautiful mother? Why hadn't his mother ever discussed his real father?

He had to know. Every thought of every day was inundated with his minds deepest unanswered questions. It became an obsession. There was no turning back. His mission was plain and simple. Find his real father and confront him with his sin of abandonment.

He was educated, intelligent and had access to all the money he wanted from his mother. She denied him nothing. His haunted mind had to be satisfied no matter what the cost. "Vengeance shall be mine," said the deserted. The shame would be on his real father. There could be no excuse for the disgrace placed upon his mother. It was a biological fact that his mother was only twelve years old at the time of conception. This fact alone made the man a pedophile in need of just punishment. Where would he start? How would he ever be able to find this needle in the pedophile haystack? All inquires; all investigation would have to be kept confidential. His mother had been hurt more than most and needed no more.

There was no secret that his mother and her brothers had spent time as "inmates" at St. Paul's orphanage. Every "inmate" had a discharge allocation sheet. Having received state and federal funds based on the US Census Bureau reports the disposition of all inmate releases had to be accounted for. A hundred dollars was a lot of money at the time. Two perhaps three months pay for a police officer. Now that his mother had purchased him the latest sports car, he simply approached a police sergeant in uniform, explained his request and drove him the fifteen minutes over to St. Paul's. The intimidated priest and nuns quickly gave up the "transfer for training purposes" record.

His birth certificate read Clarion County, PA.. By simply backdating nine months he had pinpointed the exact location where his mother was when she became pregnant. The wealth and security of the mansion's master would be a bit more difficult to crack. First he once again approached the "cop on the block" just west of the mansion. Dressed in his best suit and tie he was very soft and polite.

"Excuse me officer, do you have minute?"

"Sure son, what you need?"

"My older brother died while in the Army last year and left some money for an old girl friend who used to work at the mansion; and I'm trying to find her to give her some of the money."

"How much son?"

"Two hundred and fifty dollars, sir."

"Why don't you go straight to the mansion and ask them?"

"First of all I tried that and they said they don't give out former employee information. They were really uncooperative."

"And why do you think I can help you?"

"Well sir, everyone knows that you would know everyone and everything on your block. There can't be that many former maid employees in your domain." It was a guess but a good one. If this cop didn't help him he'd try every cop for a mile in each direction. Besides, odds were that each block had at least one former maid.

The cop thought a minute and then responded.

"How much a name and address worth to you?"

"Say twenty dollars."

"Make it twenty five and never tell anyone that I gave you the name. If you do you won't walk straight for a month."

"You've got my word and here is the twenty five."

The former maid lived a block away and hadn't worked at the mansion in over ten years. Still in his best suit and tie a very formal approach was taken.

"Good afternoon ma'am, I'm attempting to find a young lady for a small inheritance."

"Oh yes, and what is her name?"

"Rose Marie, she worked there about 18 years ago."

"I wasn't there then but I have a friend who was. She lives cross town and we still exchange Christmas cards. Here's her address, her names Anna.

Anna lived in a Southside Row house and was now married with two children. Her steel mill employed husband was at work. The knock on the door was ever so soft. Anna was now in her mid thirties, still attractive but well worn. She had a cigarette in one hand and a beer in the other.

"Good afternoon ma'am, your friend Polly said to say hello."

"Are you a friend of hers?"

"Well ma'am, we just met but she is nice."

"And what do you want with me young man?"

"Ma'am, I've got a little inheritance for a girl, now a young lady, whom you used to work for at the mansion."

"Oh yes, the mansion...what's her name?"

"Her name is Rose Marie and she'd be about thirty now. Did you know her?"

"You know, I really shouldn't be talking to you, I don't know you from blue."

"I certainly would never cause you no harm ma'am. Can you tell me anything at all about Rose? Please ma'am, I swear you'll never see me again, but please tell me what you know."

"Ok, but I'll swear you never heard it from me."

"And I also swear."

"Rose only worked at the mansion for a few months. She was a beautiful, naïve, petite thing. By her second day on the job, the master began taking advantage of her. We all figured she was with child and shipped out to keep it all hush, hush."

"Was anyone else taking advantage of her?"

"Of course not. We were all the master's private stock. All the male staff was scared shitless."

"How did you get away?"

"Just got upset when Rose got canned. A week later another young girl was brought in to replace her. A couple months later her family and some miners attacked the mansion and made a truce for some type of monthly payment."

"Did the police arrest the pervert?"

"You kidding? With all his money he owns the cops."

"Well thank you ma'am. Thank you so very much."

"Now you answer my question will you?"

"Yes ma'am, anything at all."

"How is your mother?"

Driving home in shock, he reviewed the day's events. He still had issues and unanswered questions. First he must confirm the payoff. He knew his mother kept excellent records. On Sunday while she was at Mass and Harry working, he violated her privacy for his first and last time. There it was the monthly eight dollar deposit every month right up till his eighteenth birthday. This confirmed it; he now decided to find out everything he could about his biological father.

Chapter IVX

The Untold Crime

To acquire the masters data base a systematic program was put to pencil and paper. Local libraries and newspaper archives were easily accessed. They gave a wealth of information filling in most the family and business information on the master of the house. His mother was surely not the only victim of this sick monster. Still, no criminal complaint had ever been filed.

All data traces leave tracks. A clerk at the library or inquisitive newspaper employee may wonder why the inquiry. Even a paid off cop may drop his own dime in his attempt for promotion or a gratuity. All was fair in graft and corruption. A former maid may also have loose lips which would surely help sink the mysterious Questioner. Information gathering is a two way street. There is always a weak link.

The next level of information gathering became personal. Mansion employees mostly lived in and would be difficult to interview. Factory workers would be much easier. Every company has clerks and prior to the equal rights amendments nearly all of these were young ladies still looking for a husband. He staked out the factory business office main building. Three or four young lasses were approached by the tall good looking gentleman who dressed well and drove a fine new sports car. He lied that he was doing research for a term paper at Pitt and at first only asked very basic questions, most of which he knew the answers to. He followed several home and waited for weeks to casually ask them "Didn't I see you at work at the factory?" When the answer came cordially he would dig a foot deeper, even asking some out on a date. Here he would wine and dine them for every detail he could obtain.

Once bled of all she knew he simply discarded the source. This brought discontent and hard feelings. One by one the broken hearted misses told a friend or supervisor about the inquisitive man. Corporate chains are very well lubricated. The word was on the masters desk within two weeks.

It didn't take long for the wealthy master to determine who was asking questions and why. This left more questions unanswered than answered. Sure they knew who he was, but why now, nearly twenty years after the fact? Did he want money? A piece of the inheritance? A public apology?

"We are not talking nickels or dimes. This estate is in the hundreds of millions of dollars. I will not be blackmailed."

"Butler my friend, you were probably correct twenty years ago. We should have dumped her into the river."

"Yes, but the captain of the police was present and we couldn't go against his wishes."

"That was my mistake; this is another dilemma. Is he a good kid?"

"Yes sir, tall, good looking, good grades, girls love him, dresses very well. His mother married well and money is not a problem."

"Then what does he want?"

"Seems he's an obnoxious S.O.B. with a huge ego and nasty temperament."

"Well butler, sounds like me."

Butler knew when to keep quiet.

"This time we'll do it my way. First you'll engage Pinkerton to employ a gorgeous girl his age. She'll have to be a real pro, dress college style and know her role. Then she'll have to gain his confidence and finally his plans. Of course his weaknesses will also be important. You can say she's a secretary or anything you need to, but get it done today. Let's rap this mess up this week."

"Yes sir. I'm on it."

Butler was only the procurer of the Pinkertons. This gave the master deniability and a buffer from prosecution. Pinkerton remained the premier private agency in the United States. They had also expanded into Canada and other foreign soils. This job was not so far out of line. The "Pinky" simply hired a gorgeous local lady with all the right attributes including, but not limited to, great looks, fantastic body, do anything to get the job done, excellent communication skills and best of all she knew exactly how to use the talent she was blessed with. She was lured into the job by the two best of carrots: great pay with an upfront bonus, plus expenses and a promise for a permanent career position with the Pinkertons. This first job would be not as an employee but rather as an independent contractor. Should she do a good job and be successful the greatest job with the greatest agency would be hers for life. (Or so they told her).

The target had contacted a company employee at a pub near the master's plant. Pinkerton's 'contractor' would simply be available and make her contact accordingly. Even a temp job at the plant was given the young lady as a front. She made it a point to take another young girl with her to the same pub after work on Fridays. Her target was there on each occasion but nothing was said. She was not flirtatious and sat quietly with her friend. Even when a free drink was sent over by another patron, the ladies would send it back. They were not there to be picked up but rather for a short cocktail. And short it was. Never more than one drink or three quarters of an hour were they at the pub.

This target was on a mission. He watched all the patrons as he did the main entrance to the plant. Sure enough she saw him parked nearby stalking his prey. He had no idea he was in fact the one with a bulls eye painted on his back. The sting had been set up by the best. It worked perfectly. On the third Friday the target was not at the pub. No problem, she'd simply make it next week. The target instead waited outside to follow her home to the small studio she had rented with her expense money. Part of her hiring was an agreement that she was to tell absolutely no one of her employment on the highly confidential job in which she was engaged.

He watched her on Saturday and followed her to the market as well as Sunday to church. She seemed to be a loner with no roommates or close friends. By the end of the first month he made his move at the pub. She was still with her friend.

"May I join you ladies?" said the handsome well dressed man.

"No, thank you."

"I mean you no harm, simply conversation."

"We have not been properly introduced; you could be a psycho for all we know."

"I assure you, I am not."

"No, thank you." came the stern reply.

This might be harder than he had thought. As he retreated to the bar he thought of his next move. They both obviously worked at the plant and were not easy pickups. Both were perfect for his needs for confidential, corporate information. Finally his opportunity came. On the following Friday the fine looking, conservatively dressed lady had entered the pub alone.

He slowly walked by her and stated most respectfully,

"Where's your friend?"

"Oh, she's ill today."

"Sure hate to see you sitting alone."

"Are you always here?" she inquired.

"Just on Fridays." He softly replied.

"Honestly, I never go into a bar alone and hate to sit here without someone. Seems I'm self conscious"

"I'd consider it an honor to watch over you."

So the die was set. A fine trap had been sprung by both. However she knew, he did not. He was in the grasp of the shark and the first bite would be fatal. Both took it very slow at first. A movie, a dinner and even a Sunday drive all over a thirty day span. In the second month they first kissed. He was really falling for this 'actress' who was running a con on him. She had given him a lot of facts on the company as well as answered nearly every question asked of her. Finally the necking and petting took their toll. This resulted in the ultimate love making. Even the sex was great. She was actually falling in love with him also.

The Pinkerton's 'controller' knew it was the time to strike. Their devoted undercover agent was instructed to have dinner and heavy drinking at a fine restaurant on Mt. Washington. Overlooking Pittsburgh from nearly 1000 feet above the famed Three Rivers rest many of the finest restaurants anywhere in the world. Drinks were known to be the strongest of all while the veal was (is) world renowned. They ate and drank well into the night till closing hour shut them down.

The agent had already filed her detailed final report concerning the target. He had confessed his plans to pursue his inheritance which he could easily prove. Beyond this he planned to destroy the wealthy man and use every means he could to obtain the vengeance eating at his heart. Pain of his mother would be equaled by his own plans for the pedophile. Even her reports seemed to portray her sympathy and agreement with the target. This of course was unacceptable to the powers in play. Time was of the essence. They had played far too long with this problem. Now it had to be eliminated.

She was allowing her own personal feelings to conflict with her job. Soon she'd be compromised. A compromise unacceptable to her handlers. Even in her own mind she had decided to tell him everything. The job was nearly over. Undercover work really was not her choice of vocations. Love had crept into the equation.

Love has no boundaries.

That night as they slept together she would tell him everything. But first a great meal would be enjoyed from the highest point in town. The rivers below reflected the millions of city lights. It was a lovers roost, and the main event was about to perform.

Chapter VIX

'Til Death Do Us Part

Life is a commodity we all take for granted. Of course we each have our own goals, priorities and meaning to our life. The target had confirmed his goal in life was to destroy the master. He would do this by first exposing the pedophile's sickness which would shame him in the community as well as end his marriage. Financially he would demand his total inheritance by bringing every 'rat shit' lawyer in the nation to sue the master. What the scandal failed to accomplish the lawyers' discovery should finish the job. All of this was in the girl's final report. She had no way of knowing who was the recipient of her writing or the terminal consequence of it all.

First to read the agents report was her operative. This career 'Pinky' quickly forwarded it to his regional manager. On the very same day Butler and then the master were reading the very document that could permanently harm them all. Their own life, and the stylish method of how they lived, was being seriously threatened.

"Desperate rich people do no less desperate things than do desperate poor people."

Butler made all haste in his confirmation to the 'Pinky' head to 'terminate the bastards'.

Now this may seem to be an extreme measure to many. Yet the time, circumstances and personalities involved created an unique scenario. Pinkerton's soiled history was legend. This was no big thing for the regional boss. Butler's own perversions could never be satisfied without the handsome income he had. No way would he allow his life, or his master's, to be ruined. The master himself, believing himself a

Lord and of royalty, knew in his own mind that he was correct in protecting himself, his family and his fortune. He envisioned himself above the law; the social elite and one of special privileges. He could do no wrong in his own mind.

Pinkerton's mechanic knew his job. The target's car had been parked in the paid lot across the street from the restaurant. Business was slow and the lot nearly empty. Time was not a factor. Shortly after the car was parked the 'mechanic' quickly and silently slid underneath the sports car. He had driven an older large sedan to the lot, parking it alongside the smaller sport car to shield his chore. Only the minimum of correct tools were required for this job.

As the finest veal and wine were being consumed the mechanic performed his task. Years of expert training gave him confidence as he drained all the cars brake fluid into a canning jar he had brought. This would ensure no odors or fluid discharge would be present. After ensuring the brake fluid was pumped dry he addressed the advanced progressive linkage to the carburetor. He removed the cotter pin for the linkage and replaced it with a tooth pick. This would allow the car to be started but when engaged; the tooth pick would break fully engaging the carburetor gas flow and locking the system to full maximum speed. Then the hand brake cable was cut. The mechanic's final 'fix' was the last nail for the coffin. By placing an extra hot wire from the ignition switch the electrical system would be constantly on. Of course this eventually would result in the battery going dead but this would never be an issue. Only an expert investigator could ever determine this cause of failure. Besides the difficulty in finding the hot wire, one would also be lucky if the wire was not burned or destroyed in the violent crash that would soon occur.

Pinkerton's surveillance had been relentless. They knew that their target drank heavily and drove fast. His reckless behavior would greatly aid their efforts. The sports car had a lot of horsepower which can be difficult to manage, more so when intoxicated. His car was fast, his date hot and his alcohol content triple the legal limit.

Traffic was non-existent. Their car was the only remaining in the restaurants parking lot. It was now past midnight with only a far off street light giving any light to the blackened evening. During dinner they had confirmed their love for one another and made plans to share an apartment. Even as they slowly walked their final steps across the parking lot, the smitten two exhibited the body language usually reserved for a honeymoon.

There are two primary exits off Mt. Washington. One winds down the hill and ends where the Ohio has just been formed. The other is a steep straight boulevard which dead ends where Route 51 parallels the main railroad trestle. The winding road is (was) mostly cobble stones and made for a slower rough ride. The new cement boulevard was indeed a thoroughfare built for speed. This straight steep decline is nearly a mile in length.

With the top down in the balmy evening the couple slid into the sportster while in bliss. Good food, wine and young love seems to have that effect. The car started with a roar of a lion, and then shot into first gear as if out of a canon. He took the parking lot exit without touching his brakes, shifting into second just before turning left down the steep boulevard. At sixty he did a speed shift into third and the carburetors were now stuck into maximum performance. At eighty, she screamed

"Please slow down!" To which he laughed as the night breeze and cars speed sent their hair into the nights black hole never to return.

Her fright only excited him more. His speedometer was now into the triple digits and he let off the gas pedal. To his surprise nothing happened. He immediately hit the brakes to no avail. At .30 he could not sober quickly enough. He then attempted to pull the hand brake before turning off the ignition. Nothing worked. He had to be dreaming. No way could all of these things fail at one time.

They had already passed the halfway mark and the car continued to accelerate. At 105 then 110 the telephone poles passed as toothpicks. She was screaming now with panic in her eyes.

At the bottom of the boulevard where it ends with a traffic signal for entry onto the state road, a sixteen foot reinforced concrete retaining wall supports the railroad. There is no other way out or around the 100 yard long wall.

At the very last minute he attempted vainly, to take the 90 degree turn. Instead this threw the sports car first onto its right wheels before flipping over and over then slamming full force into the solid concrete barrier. The top side hit first, crushing the occupants. The speed propelled the car's body like a large artillery shell. The resulting explosion was earth moving. Homes several miles away were shaken. Fortunately, there were no other cars involved. The first on scene could not believe their eyes. Only a few body parts and bolts remained. A mushroom cloud hung over the crash site giving off an even deadlier air. Police sirens, fire trucks and emergency crews rushed to the carnage. At first it was thought that a gas or toxic explosion might have occurred. What they found was appalling.

With auto and human body parts over 100 yards in all directions, the police and fire department began an immediate clean up. There was no reason to suspect foul play. Shortly after the crash the restaurant manager came upon the site on his way home after closing. He had observed the car screeching tires and reckless driving as he had left the customers parking lot. He also confirmed the extensive drinking and how obliviated the driver had been.

At one a.m. in the morning the police make split major decision more often than not determined by the circumstances. This tragic accident was indeed caused by alcohol and speed. Why spend half the night and all day tomorrow looking into a junked up mess that couldn't even produce a clue? And what clue? To what crime?

This was an open and shut case. The police report cited "excessive" speed and "probable alcohol" as the cause of death. Within the hour a wrecking yard towed the remains and the car was crushed the very next day. So much for the integrity of the crime scene.

Rose and the family had no reason to suspect foul play. They had no knowledge as to his personal vendetta but surely knew of his reckless driving and drinking habits.

And so the "sins, lies and untold crime of Pittsburgh".

"The Mausoleum, the DNA does not lie"

Epilogue

"Time <u>tells</u> all" is a fallacy. Time has hidden thousand of untold crimes and the criminals who committed them. Industrialist, politicians government officials and the clergy are all with sin. They more than others, due to their position in society that superficially honors their authority.

"Time heals all", is another fallacy. Rose and her family carried the loss of her only child to her grave. To those who believe "That time heals all" have them talk to a cancer or leukemia victim.

Every city has sins, lies and untold crimes. What's the solution? We can only educate our children and vote intelligently.